A MCKENZIE CHRISTMAS

MCKENZIE BROTHERS #7

LEXI BUCHANAN

HFCA Publishing House
Ireland

www.lexibuchanan.net

First Published 2015
This Edition 2024

Cover Design: Alison Chaffin Higson
Editor: Sirena Van Schaik
Editor: Nadine Winningham
BETA Reader: Emma Clifton, Lynne Garlick

SYNOPSIS

Spend December with each of the McKenzie siblings as they start their own family traditions and try to keep the romance alive with the stress of the season.

Michael and Lily struggle to find a private moment together when the twins and new baby constantly need their attention.

Sebastian is aware of something that **Carla** should have known well before him.

Ruben and Rosie discover the spirit of Christmas on the ice and move on with their lives in a surprise that Ruben has planned.

Lucien is still haunted by ghosts of his past, but with **Sabrina's** help, he's finally able to move past it.

Ramon and Noah spend the evening of their wedding preparing for their honeymoon. (MM explicit chapter)

And the **Epilogue**, well, you'll have to read the novella...

MICHAEL & LILY

MICHAEL PULLED LILY into his arms when she emerged from the nursery, having placed their two-month-old baby, Sirena, in her bassinet. "I talked to Sebastian, and we're closing McKenzie Holdings from the twenty-first until January fourth." He grinned when she looked up at him in shock. "I don't want to miss anything, and I want to be around to help you with the children." He caressed her face, captured her hands, and pulled her against his chest.

The fire in the hearth gave off a warm glow, and the crackling wood made the room cozy. It was one advantage to having an open fire, and Lily loved feeling romanced when Michael got the fire going. He always did it just for them.

Knowing that her husband still wanted to spend time alone with her and that he would do something she loved gave her a warm, fuzzy feeling. She knew he wanted to get lucky, but they could do that anywhere in the house. She just loved the romantic gesture.

"You're okay with having me underfoot?"

Lily leaned into her husband and kissed him. "Of course I am. I love having you home with us. You should know better than to ask."

You were quiet, and it had me worried." Michael slowly caressed Lily's hip as she settled against him.

"I was thinking about how much I love you," she admitted. "I don't know what I'd do without you and our children."

"I love you, too, honey." He raised his eyebrows. "I have plans for you, Mrs. McKenzie."

Lily grinned. "Is that a fact?"

"Hmm." Michael nuzzled the curve of Lily's neck and teased her with his mouth. "Don't you want to know what those plans entail?"

Lily gave a sexy laugh. "I think I have a very good idea."

Michael's fingers massaged and caressed her until she was sprawled out beneath him on the sofa. The hard ridge of his arousal pressed against her core, setting her on fire.

Her husband only had to look at her to set her body on fire. She was one lucky lady.

As she became more aroused, her nipples hardened and she felt dampness on her breasts as her milk started to leak. The only drawback to breastfeeding was that her breasts were always full of milk for Sirena, and they leaked heavily when she was aroused.

Michael shifted and captured her mouth with his, his tongue sweeping inside. His hands played along her hips and stomach, teasing her until she writhed beneath him, begging him to fill her up. As she reached up to trace a path under Michael's shirt, Sirena cried out from her bassinet.

Michael sighed, dropping his brow to Lily's chest. "I'll get her." He quickly kissed Lily before climbing off and making his way to their daughter.

As Lily straightened and rearranged her clothing, she watched as Michael gently lifted Sirena into his arms. The little one had only been asleep for thirty minutes, but even from across the room, Lily could see her chomping on her fists as she looked for milk.

The bassinet had been set up against a wall in the

living room so she would be close to her parents until they went to bed. Michael would then carry her upstairs and put her in the crib.

He sat next to his wife and tried to cradle his wiggling daughter. She wouldn't settle down; she wanted something Michael couldn't give her.

Lily knew the routine: Sirena wouldn't settle in for the night until she'd nuzzled her mother a few more times. Usually, around eleven, Sirena would have her last feeding of the night, after which she would sleep until six the next morning. Lily couldn't complain, though, because she did get unbroken sleep.

Opening her shirt, she unclipped her bra and revealed an engorged breast from which milk leaked. Sometimes she felt like a faucet with no off switch.

Michael placed Sirena in her arms. She watched his face soften as his daughter latched onto her nipple with a greedy grunt and started to nurse. Sirena's small fist rested against Lily's breast.

This time around, parenthood was different. Sirena had been breastfed at every feeding, but the twins had alternated between breast and bottle to give Lily a break.

"Do you miss being able to feed her?" Lily asked.

Something must have shown on his face. In truth, he did miss giving Sirena a bottle like he had with the twins. But how could he admit that without upsetting Lily? Upsetting Lily was the last thing he wanted to do.

"Michael, it's okay. It's written all over your face." She offered him a small smile. "I'm having trouble expressing milk, but I'm thinking about trying a bottle each evening so I can take a break. I thought you might like to give it to her."

He nodded. "I'd love that." He wrapped his arm around Lily's shoulders and cradled his daughter in her mother's arms. "I love you," he whispered into Lily's neck.

"I love you, too. Thank you for everything," she whispered, blinking back tears of happiness.

"Oh, sweetheart. It should be me thanking you." Michael kissed her on the lips and groaned when their tongues touched.

He craved intimate contact with his wife, but since she'd had Sirena, they'd only made love a few times. He was frustrated. Not just sexually frustrated, but frustrated in general.

Michael missed the alone time he used to spend with Lily before the twins were born. Even after the twins were born, they still managed to spend time alone together, and it wasn't rushed like it had become. Now that Sirena had arrived, their time together was limited. He knew Lily tried, but she was always busy with their children. He didn't blame her and knew it was just one of those things about having young children. Still, there were times when he felt lonely.

"You're frustrated," Lily observed. "I'm sorry." She sighed and wouldn't meet his gaze. "We need some time alone. Just the two of us, with no interruptions." Lily rested her head against Michael's shoulder. "I miss you."

"I can't tell you enough how much I love you. It won't always be like this. Sirena is only a few months old. She'll eventually start settling down earlier in the evening, so you won't be too exhausted to cuddle with me." Michael smiled, wanting her to know that she would always have him.

"We cuddle now, but I usually fall asleep within minutes of climbing into your arms."

He chuckled. "If it's any consolation, I'm usually not far behind you. Who knew having kids would be so exhausting?"

They chuckled together as they looked down at their sleeping daughter. It was clear that Sirena had used Lily's nipple as a pacifier.

He was uncomfortable behind his zipper. Watching his wife nurse his child was beautiful, but after she pulled the baby from her breast, her eyes dreamy with love and a soft smile on her lips, his heart stopped. The perfection of her bare breast made his fingers tingle with desire to touch it. He'd become aroused as her eyes met his, and he saw a need in her gaze. He would probably come the minute he entered her, given how aroused he was.

"Michael?" Lily pressed a hand against him.

He growled and gasped with pleasure when she stroked him. However, he didn't want to climax in his pants, which was how it was about to end.

"Don't, babe."

"But you're rock hard."

"I'll be fine." He hoped. "Let's get Sirena upstairs. It's getting late."

He stood and helped Lily to her feet, and she cradled their daughter against her chest.

Michael carried the bassinet upstairs and placed it on the stand in the corner of their bedroom. He watched as Lily bent over and put their daughter inside. Luckily, she stayed asleep.

LILY KNEW Michael was frustrated with their lack of a sex life since Sirena was born. She wished she knew how to stop it. She was exhausted from taking care of the twins and the new baby every day. Although she loved them completely, she wished she had energy left for her husband. He understood, but it hurt her as much as it hurt him.

While she'd been thinking things over, Michael got ready for bed, putting on his black pajama bottoms before climbing under the covers. Maybe tonight she could make more of an effort to stay awake.

She faced away from Michael and took a sexy babydoll nightshirt out of her drawer before going into the bathroom.

With the door closed, she quickly washed her breasts to make sure there was no lingering milk and then put on the nightshirt.

She turned and glanced at herself in the full-length mirror, and her eyes nearly popped out of their sockets. Her breasts looked huge in the outfit, spilling over the top. They were definitely bigger than before Sirena was born.

Michael loved her breasts, both before and after she had kids. He'd spend ages playing with them when they made love. She sighed. It had been a while since she'd felt close to Michael, but hopefully what she had planned was a step in the right direction.

She opened the bathroom door, took two steps into the bedroom, and then stopped short when she heard Michael snoring softly. Her eyes fixed on her husband in bed, and her heart sank. He'd fallen asleep.

Before she could cry, she quickly went into the bathroom, closed the door, and sat on the toilet seat. As her tears fell, she tried to hold back her disappointment. She felt so alone. It wasn't Michael's fault. He constantly told her he loved her and that he could wait. But she'd just discovered that she couldn't—she wanted to be with her husband and have more than just a quick coupling to satiate their lust, like it had been lately.

They needed a night together without interruptions.

After washing her face and changing into a button-down shirt for bed, she thought about everything until she finally came up with a solution.

MICHAEL HEADED DOWNSTAIRS, wondering why Lily hadn't woken him up to help with getting the children dressed and making breakfast. Instead, she'd let him sleep in until 10 a.m., which hadn't happened since before the twins were born. He'd obviously needed the sleep, but still.

Downstairs was quiet, but he heard voices coming from the living room, so he changed direction and headed that way.

He had a gut feeling that something was wrong between him and Lily. He hadn't pressured her at all about their lack of time together, whether it was for talking or more intimate activities. But something wasn't right, and he decided then and there to get to the bottom of it. The way to do that was to talk to his wife about something that didn't involve their children—well, not directly, at least.

"Michael, you sleepyhead." His mom shot up from her seat and rushed into his arms for a hug. She patted him on the back. "I can't wait for Christmas this year, with more grandchildren added into the mix."

Michael smiled at his mom's enthusiasm and met Lily's gaze over her shoulder.

"I'm looking forward to it as well."

His mom pulled back and smiled. "Go have breakfast with Lily in the kitchen while I watch these three."

He didn't move.

"Go on," she insisted and smiled.

Lily took his hand. "Come on. I have your favorite ready to reheat."

He could never say no to Lily.

"Why didn't you wake me up?" A shadow passed over Lily's face as she led him into the kitchen, but he wondered if he'd imagined it.

"You went out like a light last night, so I thought I'd let you sleep." She turned and smiled when the microwave started counting down. "I knew your mom would be here soon, so I managed." Lily walked straight into Michael's arms and held him tight.

His hands caressed her curves before settling on stroking her dark curls down her back.

LILY TOOK him in deeply and didn't want to let go when the microwave beeped, signaling that the pancakes were ready. So she didn't. They continued to hold each other in the kitchen, happy to offer each other comfort.

Unfortunately, Lily's stomach rumbled, breaking the silence.

She chuckled and stepped back. "I didn't eat with the children. I wanted to wait for you."

She placed the plate of pancakes on the table and sat beside Michael to eat. They usually sat at opposite ends of the table to make it easier to supervise the twins, but she wanted to sit close to her husband.

She'd already spoken to Pippa about leaving the children overnight sometime soon. Pippa had been giddy with excitement at the thought, but Lily wasn't sure she was ready to leave Sirena. Sirena wasn't even three months old yet, but, as with the twins, Lily felt attached to her and didn't want her or the twins out of her sight. Pippa suggested they all go somewhere together and that she'd keep the children in the room with her. That idea sounded good except it defeated the purpose of Mom and Dad having alone time. She knew she'd already made the decision to go for it because Sirena had had a bottle for breakfast.

"I've been thinking," she began, broaching the subject. "Maybe we could have a night away somewhere."

Michael stopped eating and looked so hopeful that she almost laughed.

"Maybe close by, though, in case we need to get back to the children. But I think I can manage one night." Lily met her husband's gaze.

"Are you sure you're ready to leave Sirena?" He frowned. "I remember how it took months for you to let the twins out of your sight."

"I don't think I'm as bad this time. I mean, I go shopping without her and the twins, and I'm usually only gone a couple of hours."

"This is different."

"I know it is." She smiled. "I gave Sirena a bottle while the twins ate breakfast."

Michael put his cutlery down. "You did?"

Lily nodded. "I could see your mom itching to do

it, but I told her that I wanted you to be the first person other than me to feed her."

Michael scraped his chair on the floor to get closer to his wife. Cupping her face in his hands, he said, "If you're serious about a night away, let me arrange it."

She nodded.

"I promise we'll be close to home." He kissed her on the lips.

"Just give me about a week to get Sirena used to bottles and to having someone else feed her. Hopefully, after that, we'll be good to go."

"I can do that."

"Don't you want breakfast?" Lily asked, knowing he was distracted by wicked thoughts. "Michael, they'll be cold."

"I'll enjoy them just the same."

They ate the rest of their breakfast in comfortable silence while lost in their thoughts about their night away.

IT WAS a week before Christmas and two days before her night away with Michael. Lily hurried around town to finish her Christmas shopping for the children. She rarely had time to herself. She certainly had her hands full, as she had since she met Michael. He was the love of her life, and she would be lost without him. Not a day went by without them telling each other what the other meant to them. That's why she was happy she asked him to join her for a night away. It would just be the two of them, with no one else to consider. She was nervous about leaving Sirena, but she knew her youngest daughter and the twins would be in good hands with Michael's mom.

If only she knew what to get Michael for Christmas. He was difficult to buy for, and she always struggled. He had enough money to buy whatever he wanted, which made it difficult for her to decide. One idea was to engrave their children's first initials onto gold cufflinks. Michael loved wearing his shirts to the office, but he had an assortment of mismatched ones. If that was her choice, she'd have to get a move on. Everyone would be busy, and she guessed jewelers would be too.

As she walked through the Christmas market, she spotted an old bookstall at the end of the aisle. But first, she couldn't help but stop at the display of Christmas ornaments. She loved the old-fashioned ones in red and gold. They would look amazing on their Christmas tree in the living room. Every time she sat and looked at the tree, she got tearful thinking about all the Christmases she'd missed. She couldn't imagine not having her beloved family around her. It had been so long since she'd had a family that she felt blessed to have one now.

When Michael married her, he didn't just give her his heart; he also gave her a large family, which was worth more than anything he could ever buy her. He knew that, but he loved spoiling his family, especially his wife.

Lily smiled and handed over the money for her purchases. Once she'd put them safely in her purse, she moved on to the bookstall. The man behind the counter was reading from an old book. He glanced up and smiled. "Are you looking for anything in particular?"

"Not really," Lily replied as she looked through the titles. "Maybe a Christmas book. Something we could read to our children every Christmas Eve." She glanced at the man and shrugged. "It needs to be something special."

"Hm, well, let me look." He stood up and started rooting through a box on the counter.

Lily moved over to watch him and smiled when she recognized some of the titles: Heidi, The Gingerbread Man, 'Twas the Night Before Christmas, How the Grinch Stole Christmas, and, of course, Christmas on Forty-Second Street. In the end, Lily chose an old edition of a Hans Christian Andersen book, "The Little Match Girl," for when the children were older. For now, she chose "The Snowman" by Raymond Briggs.

"I'd like these two, please." She passed her selections to the man and watched him wrap them in old Christmas paper.

"Here you go." He handed them to her, and she exchanged her money for them.

"Thank you so much." She smiled as she clutched her purchases closely. They were perfect, and she planned to leave them under the tree after the children bathed on Christmas Eve so that Michael could read them.

She had a feeling her husband would love the tradition she wanted to start. Christmases before her parents died had been huge affairs, and the whole family knew to show up—and they did. She hadn't experienced a big family Christmas again until she met Michael.

With thoughts of Michael whirling around in her head, she knew it was time to head home to her family.

EVER SINCE MICHAEL walked into Victoria's Secret with his brothers, they had been watched. Not only by the staff, but also by the other women shopping in the store. They weren't the only men in the store. Michael had never had a problem being in the store before, so he had no idea why he was having one this time. Then, as he turned around, he realized it was because he was there with Sebastian and Ruben. Lucien was due to arrive the following day with his wife and son, Alexander, for the holidays. Ramon asked why he would want something from Victoria's Secret, so he didn't come. As Michael watched Sebastian hold up panties in various colors and looked on as his brother really enjoyed himself, he couldn't help but smile.

"Hey, Michael," Sebastian shouted. "You should get Lily some of these. But if you're into ripping them off her, you should probably go for the cheaper version." He grinned.

Michael felt his cheeks redden and quickly caught the pair of pink panties Sebastian tossed to him.

He shook his head and laughed. "Behave before we get thrown out of here."

Sebastian rolled his eyes. "They won't throw us out when they want us to spend our money."

Deciding to ignore his brother, Michael looked around for Ruben and found him in one corner, looking at the babydoll dresses. Well, at least one of his brothers had the right idea.

Lily loved receiving gifts from Victoria's Secret. Normally, that wouldn't be a problem, but her breasts were at least twice their pre-pregnancy size, so he didn't know what size to buy her. He knew her bra size thanks to his snooping, but it didn't specify small, medium, or large.

His gaze soon landed on a model wearing a one-piece, but the cups of her bra gaped.

He found himself standing in front of a rack of them in various sizes. He picked up a medium, making sure the bra's cups split apart, before deciding to make the purchase. Of course, that's how his brothers found him, with his fingers wiggling through the gap.

"That's hot," Sebastian commented. "I need one of those for Carla."

Michael glanced at Sebastian, who laughed when he saw the basket brimming with underwear in his arms. "Did you destroy all your wife's things?"

Sebastian grinned. "Nearly." He walked away whistling and continued adding to his collection.

"He'll never grow up," Ruben commented, grinning. "You're just realizing that now?"

"I'm not sure about this." He held the sexy lingerie up to the window while he and his brother looked on. Imagining Lily wearing it while he stood in the store wasn't the wisest thing he'd ever done. He quickly held the basket in front of his lap and dropped the piece of lace inside. "I'm getting it. Now, for more."

As he walked off, he watched Ruben pick up the same item and put it in his basket. It appeared the outfit had affected more than just him.

"I've got some other things to do, so I'll see you later." Sebastian didn't give him time to reply before he was off and running, weighed down with bags.

Sebastian had been acting weird for a couple of days. It was as though he had a secret he was desperate to share but couldn't. He'd think more about that at some point.

It didn't take Michael long to fill his basket with panties, bras, stockings, perfume, room spray, and other things he knew Lily would love. Last year, he'd only bought her a few items from Victoria's Secret, but he knew how much she loved lingerie. That was why he'd gone all out this time. He'd pack the one-piece for their night away, though.

He couldn't wait to see her in it, but Christmas was usually hectic, so it would be a while before he could see her in his gifts. Instead of waiting, he wanted to savor her while he had her all to himself.

"LILY, WE CAN CALL AGAIN." Michael knew Lily was having a hard time relaxing because she missed having Sirena in her arms.

"No, your mom has our numbers, as well as the hotel's, so I'm sure she'll call if there's a problem." She smiled, and her whole face lit up. "No matter how much I fret, I want you to know how much it means to me that we're alone tonight. I've missed you so much."

"Oh, babe." Michael pulled her into his arms and held her close. He'd planned on taking her out to dinner, but if they continued, they'd have to order room service much later in the evening. "I've always been right in front of you, just like you have with me."

Michael picked Lily up and stepped back to sit on the sofa in their hotel suite. "Lily, I love you. I know things have been difficult with three kids under three, but I'm not going anywhere. You'll always have me, even when I'm a frustrated dick."

Lily started to chuckle, which eventually turned into a fit of laughter. "Frustrated dick? Do you get it?"

Michael grinned and admitted, "Well, I guess that was an accurate description."

"Let's not go out to eat. I want to stay here, just the two of us. I want to make love all night."

Michael was certainly up for that.

"I have something for you," he said. Just the thought of seeing Lily in the lace he'd bought made his dick ache.

"An early Christmas present?" Lily sat up and her eyes sparkled as they widened when she felt the rock beneath her.

She wiggled as he gripped her hips and held her still. "I want you so badly that if you wiggle a few more times, I'll come in my pants."

"Mmm."

"Lily," he growled, putting her on her feet. Michael followed and retrieved his gift from his overnight bag, where he'd hidden it.

He held it out to Lily with one finger. She had a secret smile on her lips as she took it from him.

"I'll change in the bathroom."

Michael sighed in relief once his wife was out of view. He hadn't lied about coming in his pants. He was so hard that Lily was lucky he hadn't tackled her to the floor.

While she was in the bathroom, he quickly stripped and sprawled out on top of the bed to wait for her, naked.

His cock throbbed for relief, and his arousal dripped from the plump crown to his stomach. He was tempted to masturbate before she appeared so that he would have some control. He knew it would only take a few strokes before he came.

Too late, though.

The door opened slowly, and Lily stood in the doorway of the bathroom, arms crossed, looking unsure.

Michael smiled and tried to hold himself in check at the sight of his beautiful wife. She made his heart beat wildly and his dick jerked as though it had received an electric shock. Soon, Lily would find out just how desperate he was for her when he came without touching himself.

He closed his eyes, but that didn't calm him down. If anything, it made it worse. So, when he opened his eyes and saw Lily still standing in the doorway, he said, "Drop your arms. I want to see all of you."

She hesitated, biting her lip, before dropping her arms.

He couldn't catch his breath as she bared her breasts and walked forward. They swayed as she walked; her nipples were large and dark, hard and prominent. He couldn't take his eyes off her as his dick bounced with excitement.

He was about to come.

He scooted to the end of the bed, reached for Lily, and impaled her. The head of his penis hit her cervix —he was that deep. Still unable to catch his breath, he felt Lily press her breasts against his chest. He started to come. His hands flexed on Lily's hips as he ground into her. His semen wouldn't stop, and then he felt her walls ripple along his length. She gasped, moaning into his neck as her orgasm claimed her. She milked him, not letting up until one last burst of semen shot out. They collapsed against each other, and she kissed his jaw.

"Wow, we were both starved, huh?" Lily giggled.

"Fuck me," Michael murmured as he held his wife tightly in his arms.

He was still hard inside her. With some maneuvering, he managed to get them further up the bed, his dick still buried in her hot sheath.

As he loomed over her, he gently rocked back and forth, creating delicious friction inside her. Lily had no idea Michael was so turned on that he would come the minute he was buried deep inside her. In fact, she'd had no idea that she was ready to climax with him so quickly.

She was surprised by the outfit Michael had bought her, but she really shouldn't have been because he loved her teasing him. The outfit certainly did that, with split cups over her breasts. Lily was lucky because her breasts had stayed firm, even though they had grown drastically since she'd been pregnant with Sirena. Of course, they held milk for their daughter, but Michael was a breast man, so no doubt they did things to him that he'd never admit to her—or would he?

"I take it you like the outfit." She grinned up at him.

"Yes," he croaked, his eyes fixed on her breasts, which were still bursting free of the outfit.

She laughed, her eyes sparkling with mischief as she teased him. She licked her finger, then traced a path down to her nipple and flicked it over the sensitive flesh. Lifting both arms, she stared into his eyes as she cupped her breasts with her hands. Her thumbs rubbed back and forth over her engorged nipples, drawing a moan from her. They felt wet, which told her that some milk had leaked, but it felt too good to stop. Her channel fluttered around Michael's thick shaft as she continued teasing him. It wasn't long before he lost control, dipping his head to sample her nipples.

"I have months of built-up lust for you, dear wife. I hope you're ready for me." He swirled his tongue around one of her nipples as he slid a hand under her ass and held her against him as he thrust.

She groaned, trying to control her breathing. With Michael setting her senses on fire, however, she had no chance. But she wouldn't go over alone. Her hands reached out and her fingers tangled in his hair as he continued to lap at her breasts.

Lily wrapped her legs around his waist and thrust her hips up into him. Michael growled and met her gaze.

"I love you." He reared up, wrapped her in his arms, and slowed his pace. "No matter what. No matter how much time goes by between us making love, I love you. Always."

Lily felt tears fill her eyes at her husband's beautiful words. That's what she needed to hear, and he didn't disappoint.

He bent down, kissing the tears away while never stopping his slow movements inside her.

Lily reached up and cupped his face in her hands. "You're always in my thoughts, even when I'm tired from spending all day with the children. You're my heart, Michael."

"Damn straight." He sealed their lips together in a kiss that said more than words ever could.

Then, he made love to his wife for the rest of the night.

SEBASTIAN & CARLA

CARLA SIGHED as she glanced around the room, feeling proud. Their cabin looked festive now that they had spent a couple of days setting up the tree and decorations. She felt happy. Like, really happy. For the first time in years, her brother Noah would be there to celebrate the holiday with her. Not only would she have her husband, Sebastian, and his family on Christmas Day, but she would also have what remained of her own family.

Nothing would prevent them from having the perfect Christmas. Last Christmas with Sebastian had been perfect, but this year, she wouldn't have to worry about whether her brother was still alive.

Sebastian made her feel like she could accomplish

anything she set her mind to, and he encouraged her like no one else could. He acted like a big kid most of the time, but she loved him.

Her husband was currently messing about in the attic of their cabin. She loved the sprawling, ranch-style house, but because of its wooden exterior, she couldn't bring herself to call it a house. She preferred to call it a cabin.

He was up to something, though. He had placed all her presents under the tree before she had even put up a single decoration on the green spruce. But he was acting weird, for want of a better word. It was as though he had a secret or surprise he was dying to reveal. She knew he could be difficult when he knew something that no one else did. This time, however, she felt it was more than that.

This time, he'd actually used the excuse of finding more Christmas decorations to go into the attic. She didn't believe him and knew that she'd soon have him pinned down, naked and wild with lust for her. When she did, she'd tease him until he admitted what was going on. She wasn't really a tease because Sebastian usually didn't last very long. But she could do it. She hoped. She'd have fun doing it as well.

"Hey, babe. Look what I found!" Sebastian walked

into their living room, and Carla laughed as she looked at her husband. He looked like a ghost, covered in dust.

Carla couldn't make out what he was holding, so she crossed the room and peered into his arms. Upon closer inspection, she saw that he was holding a kitten.

"Please tell me you didn't find that little thing in the attic." She took the kitten from Sebastian and cuddled it close. Its little meows tugged at her heart-strings.

"No, I didn't find anything up there but rubbish." He wouldn't meet her gaze. "I went to put some of it outside and found this one in a tree."

"Oh, no. I bet you're hungry," she muttered to the kitten as she went to find some milk. She didn't have any cat food, but she could get some later. They ate meat, though, so she was sure Sebastian wouldn't mind sharing his beef fillet with the little thing.

As he watched Carla tend to the kitten he had found, he sighed with relief, knowing he had found a distraction. She was on to him and knew he was up to something. He hated keeping something from her, but sometimes the woman was clueless. All she had to do was open her eyes.

He grinned as Carla stood in front of him with the kitten curled up in her hand, and he raised his eyebrows at her. "So, what name have you given it?"

She narrowed her eyes. "Are you sure you found this in a tree?"

"Of course I did."

"Sebastian—"

"Carla." He chuckled. "I promise I found it in a tree. If I had bought it for you for Christmas, I would have said so. I mean, I'd want credit for making you smile."

"Okay, I believe you."

Sebastian lived to make her smile, and he hated it when she was under the weather. Sometimes, Carla teased him, saying that he fussed over her more than his mother did.

"So, have you named her yet?" He grinned.

She shook her head and laughed. "Buttons."

"Buttons? What kind of name is that?" He grumbled as he followed her back into the living room.

"It's a good name. The little thing is white except

for the black dot on her nose. I'd rather call her Buttons than Dot."

Sebastian rolled his eyes. "Now you're just being ridiculous."

Carla snickered. "I learned from the best and the most handsome."

"Hmmm, buttering me up will get you everything."

"I don't need to butter you up," she said, stepping into his space and curving her free hand around his neck. "I know you love me as much as I love you."

"I love you more." He grinned and stole a quick kiss, knowing the argument would go on forever if he let it.

Carla's eyes filled with heat before she gave him a heart-stopping smirk that made him think naughty thoughts. "I'm not getting into that right now. We can argue about that when we're both naked and you're begging me to have sex with you," she purred.

Sebastian hardened at her words, wondering if they could sneak in a quickie before his dad arrived to help him move the huge tree from his truck to the hole in front. The ground was frozen, so he borrowed some heavy equipment from one of the McKenzie construction sites to dig it out. His nearest and dearest had admitted that she'd always wanted a

Christmas tree outside covered in lights. So, of course, he bought the biggest one he found at the lot. He still wondered if he'd have to call Ramon and Noah to help because the tree was extremely heavy.

"That will be your dad," Carla grinned.

"He has bad timing," he grumbled.

"No, he doesn't. I'm impatient to decorate and light the tree." Carla was so excited about the tree that she made Sebastian forget about his hard-on, and he grinned with her.

"I'll find out how to get the tree off my truck while you find a secure place to keep Buttons."

Carla reached up and whispered against his lips, "I love you." She sealed his response in his mouth with a kiss, which turned into a groan when she gave him her tongue.

His hand grabbed her ass and pulled her hard against him. Suddenly, a meow broke them apart. They had nearly crushed the kitten between them.

Sebastian groaned, adjusted himself, and, after kissing his wife quickly, headed outside.

"I'M glad I picked up your brother and Noah," his dad commented, staring at the tree. His hands were firmly planted on his hips, and he had a sour frown on his face.

Sebastian stood beside his dad and looked at the tree as well. It wouldn't be too bad, really, except the trunk was thick and large enough to make it cumbersome to move.

Ramon nudged Sebastian, who laughed when he noticed the same expression on his brother's face.

"Can't we split it in half?" Ramon asked, not at all helpfully.

"Did you come to help plant the tree or drink coffee with my wife?" Sebastian grumbled.

Ramon grinned and glanced toward the house. Sebastian sighed as his brother and Noah ran away from the tree and up the steps to the cabin. Their father laughed as the door slammed shut behind them. Sebastian grinned back at his dad. His brother and Noah wouldn't be inside long because Carla wanted the tree up soon. There'd be no coffee or cookies until the tree was planted.

"We'll wait for the kids to come back out here, and then we'll get it out, son." His dad rubbed his shoulder in a gesture that was all too familiar. He was a man of few words, but he had been doing that since Sebastian was little. He grew up to realize that it was his father's way of showing his love. They all relished it.

"I'm surprised you had time to come down here. Doesn't Mom have you running around like usual?" His mom was really the glue that held the family together. She welcomed Carla and each of his brothers' girlfriends without hesitation.

He shook his head. "She's baking up a storm in the kitchen with Rosie, and apparently, I was in the way." He chuckled. "I think what she meant when she said I needed to find something to do was that I needed to stop eating the snickerdoodles."

Sebastian straightened up from where he was slouched against his truck. "Snickerdoodles? Mom made snickerdoodles, and you didn't bring any?"

"Son, you know how your mother is when she has her mind set. They're for Christmas Day. So it's either hands off or get an apron to help replace the ones in your stomach."

Sebastian laughed. "I can't believe Mom would suggest you help bake."

"Me either, son. I think it was a ruse to get me out of there. Girl talk and all that."

"Rosie's okay, right?"

"I think so. She had a beautiful smile on her face when I saw Ruben drop her off. I actually thought they'd be hooking up in his car outside the front door." His dad chuckled. "If there is something going on, it isn't between the two of them."

"Okay, here they come." He was referring to Ramon and Noah, but he laughed when he saw his wife shaking her head in the background at something Noah said.

"Are you annoying my wife?"

"Nope." Noah grinned. "I was annoying my sister." He smirked.

"Ass."

"Okay, boys. I have better things to do today than stand around and listen to you argue." At least their father managed to shut them up.

After about ten minutes of debating the best way to plant the tree, they tied a rope around it and, using their combined strength, dragged it from the bed of the truck. It was no easy task because it weighed a ton. At least it was out now. Now, they just had to plant it so his wife could decorate it. Not that she was going up any ladders—he would do that part.

"We've got this," his dad said as they struggled to

keep the tree upright while dropping it into the hole he'd dug.

By the time they were done, they were all sweaty, but Sebastian had to admit that the tree looked good. Hopefully, it would continue to grow and stay healthy, since most of its roots were still attached. He sure as hell didn't plan on doing this every December.

"I think we all deserve coffee and cake. Carla baked them earlier as a treat for putting up the tree." Sebastian chuckled, though, when he realized he had spoken to their backs. They were already on their way inside.

You'd think they hadn't eaten. He didn't know a McKenzie who would refuse homemade cake.

"WHERE DID YOU PUT BUTTONS?" Sebastian asked as he walked into his bedroom and didn't see his wife.

Carla chuckled from the en suite bathroom. "Sebastian McKenzie, you are such a softie."

He followed her voice and instantly became aroused when he found her naked, having just gotten out of the shower. As she turned to hang the towel back on the rack, he pressed up against her ass and held her close with his arm around her stomach. "There's nothing soft about me, baby." He nuzzled his face into the curve of her neck, and he was in heaven. The woman in his arms meant the world to him. She was his everything.

"She's in the bathroom down the hall with her litter box, food, and water. She'll be fine." She pressed her ass against his groin and rubbed. "Mmm, Sebastian," she sighed.

His breath caught in his throat as arousal shot through him, and he reached up to cup her breasts. They were firm and filled his hands. Her nipples hardened under his touch, and his dick throbbed behind his zipper.

Carla always made him feel like a horny teenager who constantly wanted to get off. If he could, he would be naked with her every minute of every day.

"Bed." He pinched her nipples. "Now."

Without giving her a chance to move, he picked her up and carried her to their huge bed, laying her beneath him.

He found it sexy to be fully clothed while she wasn't. He was wearing sweats and a T-shirt, yet he could feel every contour of her nude body against him. One particular part of him was hard as steel, pressing against her soft thigh. With a pulse of its own, it throbbed.

She helped him pull off his T-shirt, and when he smiled down into her eyes, he showed her all the love he felt for her.

She reached up, cupping his face and stroking his lips with her thumb. "Make love to me."

"Always." He bent down and captured her lips.

As their tongues swirled together, she urged his sweats past his hips. Then, she used her feet to push them down his legs.

He groaned when, with her movements, his dick took up residence between her thighs, his balls pressing against her wet pussy. He promised himself that one day he would have enough control over his body's reaction to his wife that he would last all night. But as he looked down at her, all he wanted was to be buried deep inside her warmth.

He grinned, dipping down to capture one of her dark nipples in his mouth before kissing his way down her body. He nuzzled her stomach, kissing the sensitive skin, and inhaled her scent.

He lay flat on his stomach between her thighs and buried his face in her pussy. She was so wet for him, and he knew she wanted more. Her legs rested on his shoulders, and nothing felt better than where his tongue was about to go.

It was his first taste of her in over a day, and he couldn't control the urge to rock his hips. Her nectar coated his tongue, and his dick tingled and dripped precum between his belly and the bed. He didn't stop, though.

SEBASTIAN HAD A WICKED TONGUE, and the minute he touched her, Carla's senses swam. She gripped the quilt beneath her and prayed he would let up, even though she knew he wouldn't. Her husband loved having his face between her thighs, and on a few occasions, he had climaxed while bringing her to orgasm.

His tongue and fingers sent her into bliss within seconds, and today was no exception.

His hands curved under her buttocks to hold her open, and then his eyes met hers. She knew that look. He wanted to watch her fall apart on his mouth.

She cupped her breasts and rolled and pinched her nipples as Sebastian's eyes darkened with lust. She didn't miss the way his hips constantly rolled into the bed.

"Inside me," she gasped, changing her mind. "Oh God, Sebastian. I want you to come inside me. Now."

Her husband surged up as if his ass were on fire and thrust into her. She didn't have time to catch her breath before their lips sealed and her vaginal walls began milking Sebastian's release.

They groaned and gasped, and Carla couldn't stop her pussy from clenching around Sebastian's cock. She felt his hot seed fill her up, setting her off again. She screamed her ecstasy into his mouth. Her pussy and breasts were more sensitive than ever before. Even when Sebastian tried to ease her down with slow thrusts, her body trembled and rippled against him. Their gazes met and held as her slow blast of ecstasy washed over them both.

Sebastian was still hard inside her, but Carla had no idea how he'd find the energy for another round. Her orgasm had lasted longer than any before, and it had felt amazing. Her pussy pulled on her husband's hard flesh, making him come hard and long. In fact, he'd released so much semen that she could feel it running out of her as he moved slowly inside her.

"Fuck," Sebastian finally breathed, dropping his head to her shoulder. "You nearly killed me."

She tried to pull him down on top of her, but instead, he rolled onto his side and pulled one of her legs over the curve of his hip to keep them together.

"I have no words."

"You milked everything out of me, babe."

She smiled against him while he made sure she was comfortable. Then he mumbled, "Go to sleep."

She felt him slip out of her just as she drifted off to sleep.

"HOW ARE YOU FEELING?" Sebastian asked on the way to the doctor's office.

Carla gave him a weak smile, but it was short-lived. She turned green before his eyes. She twisted toward the window, rolled it down, and drew in a deep breath of crisp, fresh air. "I'm okay. I just get a little carsick," she said when her color finally returned.

Sebastian nodded and took her hand as he pulled into the parking lot. He didn't say anything, but he was sure he knew what was wrong with her, even if his clueless wife didn't. Or at least he hoped he was right about what was wrong. Despite her brave front, Sebastian knew Carla must be worried. This morning, when he brought up the idea of going to the doctor, Carla had agreed, which was unlike her. There was no way Carla would go to the doctor if she thought she just had a cold.

"I'm not too bad now. At least, I don't think I am." She chewed her lip and met his gaze. "Perhaps we should go home. She's probably busy, and it was probably something I ate."

"No, we're here now, so we might as well get you checked out." Besides, you didn't eat anything last night, so it can't be something you ate. You would have been sick last night if that were the case."

"True."

He knew his wife hated going to the doctor and that she wanted to stay home. But she'd felt unwell for a few mornings now, and he wondered...

"We're here," he announced unnecessarily since the elevator had stopped and the doors had opened.

"Maybe the doctor needs to check you out because you're acting strange," Carla said dryly.

He smiled but didn't rise to her bait. "No stranger than usual, babe."

She raised an eyebrow in his direction before they were interrupted.

"Hello, Mr. and Mrs. McKenzie. The doctor is waiting for you both." The receptionist seemed pleasant enough.

He held the door for her, and as they walked inside, the doctor got to her feet. "Carla, come in and have a seat."

Being in the room always made him nervous. He had no idea why, since he'd never had a bad experience at the doctor's office.

He took his wife's hand when he sat beside her and gave it a reassuring squeeze. He wasn't sure how he was going to ask the doctor to give her the test he wanted.

"So, what's the problem?"

"I've been unwell," Carla began. "Actually, it's been about two weeks that I haven't felt that great."

"She felt sick this morning," he chimed in.

The doctor met Sebastian's gaze, and her eyes widened when she realized why they had the appointment. Sebastian shook his head slightly when the doctor glanced at Carla and then back at him.

The doctor coughed as though she needed to clear her throat and hid a smile behind her hand. "Okay, then. I'd like to run some bloodwork, and I'd like you to provide a urine sample. There are cups in the restroom that you can use. Leave the sample with the nurse when you're ready."

Carla nodded as the doctor checked her blood pressure and temperature. After jotting down a few notes, she said, "Go give me a urine sample, and then we'll draw your blood," before slipping out the door. Sebastian could barely keep his excitement under control.

"Sebastian?" Carla murmured. "You seem too happy about me being sick."

"Shush, babe. Everything will be fine. Just go in there, drop your panties, and get it over with." He smirked.

Carla smacked his arm. "Drop my panties? What's wrong with you?"

"Honey, that's the only way you're going to pee in the cup."

"Ugh! I knew I should have come on my own," she mumbled as he watched her disappear inside the restroom.

Perhaps it hadn't been a good idea to tell her to drop her panties. All he could picture was her silky-smooth ass as he pounded into her while she was on her hands and knees.

His brothers always teased him about always thinking about sex, and for the first time, he actually agreed with them.

AFTER GETTING A SAMPLE, Carla slipped into the nurse's office and had her blood drawn. Then, they went back into the small room. They sat together as Sebastian held her hand. Each was lost in their own thoughts as they waited. Fifteen minutes felt like forever, but the doctor slipped back into the room soon after.

"We have everything we need from you, but I'll need you to schedule some follow-up appointments." The doctor stared down at her tablet as she read Carla's file. Carla was filled with panic...more appointments! What was wrong with her?

When the doctor looked up and smiled, relief flooded through Carla. It couldn't be anything too serious if she smiled like that, which probably meant...

"And I see that congratulations are in order."

Carla's mouth dropped in surprise as she whispered, "What?" She knew what the doctor meant, but her brain wasn't processing the words.

"You're pregnant."

Carla felt her face drain of color at the doctor's words, and her mind whirled around the fact. How was it possible? She was on the pill so she and Sebastian could enjoy having sex without a condom. Besides, she loved it when he came inside her, so they hadn't used anything for a while. But pregnant?

"How exactly did that happen?"

Carla's question wiped the smile off Sebastian's face. However, he answered with amusement, "If the doctor wasn't here, I'd show you."

Carla groaned and smiled. She beamed when she realized that Sebastian was happy about the pregnancy. But then another thought hit her: "Wait a minute." She narrowed her eyes at Sebastian. "How did you know I was pregnant?"

"I didn't," he began, then stopped and admitted, "Okay, I did. After you felt off a couple times, I realized it was always before lunch. So, I put two and two together." He grinned.

She had questions for Sebastian, but she wanted to

talk to him in private. For now, the doctor was enjoying their discussion.

"Now that the shock has worn off, how are you feeling?" Sebastian asked.

She didn't know how to answer because they needed to talk. Until they did, she wouldn't be able to answer.

They had talked about having kids before, but they agreed to wait a few years so they could spend time together on their own first. Carla's pregnancy threw things off kilter.

"I'm not sure." She was honest. "How do you feel?"

He stared at her before asking again. "I want to know how you feel, babe."

"Stop doing that!" she snapped. "I seriously want to know how you feel about us being pregnant. I know I'm the one carrying our child, but it involves both of us, and it always will."

Sebastian perched on the coffee table in front of his wife, who was curled up in a chair in the living room. He placed his hands on her thighs. "Carla, I love you with everything I have. I will love and protect any child we have together. I know this baby is coming a bit earlier than we planned, but you asked for the truth, and the truth is, I'm excited to become a father. There's nothing sexier than knowing the woman I love is carrying my child."

"Really?" Carla had tears running down her face at Sebastian's sweet words.

He pulled his wife out of her chair, sat back down, and pulled her into his lap so he could hold her close. He kissed her forehead and asked, "Will you tell me what you're thinking and how you feel?"

"I was shocked, to be honest, when the doctor announced that I was pregnant. But when I looked at you and saw your love, I felt a bubble of excitement start to grow inside me. Until I was told that a baby was growing inside me, I didn't know just how much I wanted to be a mom." She smiled through watery eyes. "I love you."

Carla started kissing her way across his jaw and neck before straddling him. She rubbed up against his erect penis, and he froze.

"Fuck."

"What?"

"I never asked the doctor if we could still have sex." He paled, and Carla laughed.

"Don't be silly. Of course we can have sex. In fact, it was probably my changing body that caused my reaction when I came the other night."

"So that wasn't a one-off?"

"I don't think so." She grinned, knowing where his thoughts were headed.

Before she could catch her next breath, She was in his arms, being carried to the bedroom.

She didn't miss the little "meows" coming down the hallway as he paused in the doorway to their room.

"Oh, fuck it." He cursed and left the door open so the kitten could come and go as it pleased.

3

RUBEN & ROSIE

IT WAS the middle of the week, so Kenza wasn't as busy, which was just fine because Rosie was desperate to get her husband to dance with her. She just wanted to be in his arms, and that would be a good enough excuse. She didn't need an excuse, but since they were supposed to be working, they preferred to keep things professional. However, it was almost Christmas, so they could try something different.

Her husband hated dancing, which surprised her at first, considering he owned one of the hottest nightclubs in Lexington. She had plans for the evening, though, which involved being on the dance floor in his arms.

She had already talked to the DJ about what music

to play when they were on the dance floor, so her plans were set. All she needed was her husband, who was busy in his office sorting out the payroll so all his employees would be paid before Christmas. No matter how many times Ruben told her it was "their" business as opposed to "his" business, Rosie still couldn't bring herself to call it theirs. She knew it bothered him, but it made her uncomfortable. Perhaps in time "theirs" would come more easily.

They hadn't been married that long, but not a day went by without her waking up in Ruben's arms. He had been under her skin since the day they met, and her desire for him knew no bounds. In fact, she'd come a long way in learning to trust Ruben completely. He often showed her that he trusted her just as much by allowing her to do things to him.

"What has your cheeks rosy, Rosie?" Scott grinned. He'd been working behind the bar for about two months now, and he had potential as a bartender. He loved to tease her, and Ruben only allowed it because they both knew he was gay and practically married to his boyfriend. "Or don't I want to know?"

She smirked. "You probably don't want to know."

"Hmm, one of those thoughts, huh?" He put some glasses on the cleaned shelf and turned back to look at her. "Then again, if your thoughts involve that hot piece you're married to, I could listen."

Rosie narrowed her eyes, telling him to be quiet. She knew he liked Ruben, but she also knew how much he was in love with Burt, his partner.

"Looks like lover boy has dug himself out of his books." Scott nodded.

Rosie knew her face lit up as soon as she focused on her handsome husband. She also recognized the look on Ruben's face as he walked toward her. It was the look that said he meant business—the hot-and-bothered kind.

She met him halfway, sighing in pleasure when he curved his arm around her waist and pulled her close. He cupped her chin with his other hand and tilted her face up so he could take her in. He smiled at what he saw before capturing a kiss from her.

HE LOVED WORKING alongside his wife and couldn't go more than an hour without seeing her. Knowing she was in the same room helped him get through his day. She certainly had a habit of distracting him, especially when they worked in his office alone together.

It probably wasn't the best time to think about being alone with his sexy wife.

"Dance with me."

He wanted to say yes, but he couldn't dance. His two left feet made sure of that. But as he looked at Rosie, he knew what his answer would be.

He smiled, kissed her lips, and led her to the dance floor. The minute they stepped onto the dance floor, the music changed. He didn't roll his eyes, but he did chuckle when Ed Sheeran's "Thinking Out Loud" blared through Kenza. Rosie loved dancing around their apartment with a broom to that song.

She had always felt right in his arms, against his body. As he held her close with their foreheads touching, he found it difficult to imagine life without her. She was beautiful, inside and out. Her heart was big, which caused him great frustration on occasion. Once she had an idea, nothing could sway her off course.

He swept the imaginary hair from her face and dipped down to kiss her. He often struggled to walk past her without quickly kissing her.

"Mmm, I think someone's hoping to get lucky later," Rosie said, nuzzling against him and sighing in pleasure as her hand landed on his butt.

Groaning, Ruben replied, "If you keep doing that, we're going to get it on sooner rather than later."

She teased him more, rubbing against his awakening cock. "I have this fantasy," Rosie began. She smiled when Ruben shuddered against her. "Of you being naked and tied to your office chair." She nibbled his earlobe and trailed her tongue along his jaw. Her hand caressed his spine and moved toward his ass. "Mmm, so hot."

Rosie loved to tease Ruben, and she always got his motor running. He was hard as steel inside his pants, and she knew it.

Breathing heavily, he met her gaze and changed the subject before he embarrassed himself in front of his club members: "We need to talk more about what kind of house we're looking for." They had only recently discussed contacting a realtor, but then he found out that the house Rosie loved had been put on the market. He had plans, but he had to keep them from his wife for just a little while longer.

"I know." She kissed his chest. "We can discuss that in your office and play afterwards. Although, I'll probably spend the whole time imagining you naked and what I'm going to do to you."

Ruben narrowed his eyes. "Babe, you won't last long enough to do much to me."

Wasn't that the truth? They both craved each other, and neither had learned patience yet.

"You want to talk now?" Ruben asked, impatient to get to the part of the evening where Rosie was tied to a chair.

"In a few minutes," Rosie mumbled into his neck. "I love being in your arms on the dance floor. We don't do this enough."

Her comment reached him where it hurt. He hated dancing; he had no rhythm. Before their wedding, he'd taken lessons with Rosie, and he'd managed not to embarrass himself, but the music in Kenza was different. The club's patrons loved the music and came back week after week for more. It just wasn't something he ever felt brave enough to try until Rosie came along.

The slower song was easy to dance to with his love in his arms. No one would know that Rosie led, nor that he wanted to make love to his wife with the kind of desperation only she brought out in him.

If he didn't stop thinking with his penis, he'd be as bad as his brother Sebastian. Ruben wasn't sure his brother would ever grow up.

As he thought of the quickest way to get Rosie off the dance floor, he felt her body grow heavy and lethargic. He gazed into her eyes and knew she was getting sleepy in his arms. He could try to curb the lust he always felt for her. Couldn't he?

"Rosie?" he whispered in her ear.

"Hmm."

He grinned. "You mean to tell me you've gotten me all worked up, and now you're about to fall asleep?"

She groaned. "In five seconds, I'm going to fall asleep on my feet."

"I know." He sighed, but a grin split his face. She was his, and if she was tired, he would wait until morning.

He kissed her forehead before picking her up. "Your shift is over, babe."

Her arms slipped around his neck. "I love you."

As he strolled toward the stairs that led to their apartment, he whispered against her lips, "I love you, too." His lips quickly descended, and she fell asleep in the warmth of his embrace.

HIS WIFE HAD a smirk on her face, telling him that she was up to something. But what? She'd fallen asleep on her feet the previous night, and he'd gotten up to accept a delivery before she woke up. When he came back upstairs, Rosie was already showered and dressed because he'd taken longer than usual downstairs.

She placed his breakfast in front of him, along with a steaming mug of coffee, and took her seat opposite him. For the past five minutes, she had sat and watched him eat. It killed him to carry on as normal when he itched to laugh and give in to her.

It wasn't until he felt her foot beneath the leg of his jeans that he finally cracked a grin. "Okay, babe. You win. What are you up to?"

Rosie shrugged. "Who, me? I'm not doing anything."

She gave up on trying to unbutton his jeans and settled for running her foot up his leg. As her foot crept closer to his groin, his dick perked up, and he spread his thighs, giving her easy access.

"Are you aroused, baby?" Rosie mumbled in a sultry voice, her foot hovering inches from his groin.

"Why don't you stop teasing and find out?"

Rosie tipped her head back and laughed throatily.

"Oh, you're aroused. I know without even touching you."

He groaned and stared at his teasing wife, narrowing his eyes.

"I think," she said, standing up, "that you need to follow me back to bed."

Did he have time? Another delivery was due in fifteen minutes.

Fuck it.

He stood and stalked toward Rosie, who had a come-hither look on her beautiful face.

Before he could grab her and throw her over his shoulder, she dropped to her knees and started fiddling with his belt.

His dick lengthened with arousal even as he said, "Rosie, not here." The view of Rosie on her knees excited him. Then he nearly dropped to the floor when her wet mouth surrounded the head of his dick.

She was so good at sucking him off, and he never lasted more than a minute or two. But when she took him further inside, he saw stars and tried to pull out.

"No," Rosie argued, wrapping her fist around him. "I want to suck you off before we go ice skating." She smirked and pulled back to the base of his penis.

As he looked down, he saw the head bulge and drip

precum. The sight and then the feel of her tongue sent a bolt of pleasure through his body. Her fingers pressed between his legs, and she massaged his scrotum with her palm. Her other hand tightened around his shaft as she jerked him off quickly and sucked him.

His hands tangled in Rosie's hair, and, as he watched her head bob back and forth on his shaft, he couldn't hold on anymore. She excited him too much.

Ruben groaned and warned, "Rosie, I'm gonna come."

She grunted in acknowledgment, and then he slipped further. That was all it took; he came down her throat. He tried not to thrust and choke her, but she wouldn't let up. Finally, she settled on cleaning his dick after he came.

On her knees, Rosie grinned up at him as his dick started to swell with new arousal. He chuckled and pulled his jeans up before pulling his wife into his arms.

They sealed their mouths together, letting their tongues caress each other with the love they shared. He couldn't get enough, but when Rosie broke the kiss, he suddenly remembered what she'd said.

"Ice skating?"

Rosie chuckled. "I wondered when what I said would register."

"Now, babe. I love you, but I'll only embarrass you." He kissed her and tried to push her into the bedroom.

She slipped out of his arms and quickly moved to the door, where she started to pull on her jacket and boots. "Ruben, you know how much I love winter with snow and ice skating." She grinned. "And you won't embarrass me at all."

Could he put on skates without looking foolish? He had no balance and always ended up injured when he skateboarded as a kid. His brothers used to tease him relentlessly.

Rosie stood in front of him, holding his jacket and hat. "Humor me. If you really don't want to go on the ice when we get there, we can just walk around the park and the Christmas market, drinking hot chocolate." She smiled the smile she knew he could never resist. "I even talked Scott into coming in today to look after the deliveries you're expecting. You know Scott knows what he's doing." He's done it on more than one occasion. So, Mr. Control-Freak, you have most of the day off." She grinned, and he could tell she really wanted him with her. How could he possibly refuse? He couldn't.

He smiled to let her know that he was okay with her sneakiness. "I love you." He planted a hard kiss on her lips, grabbed his jacket and hat from her hands, and moved toward the door. Over his shoulder, he asked, "Coming?"

Rosie cocked an eyebrow and smirked. "Not yet, but I will be tonight."

He raised an eyebrow and grinned. "Wife, if you want to go to that place you have your heart set on, I suggest you keep those ideas to yourself for now."

She giggled and jumped into his arms. "I love you. Let's go."

As THEY WALKED through the market, snow fell around them, and Rosie couldn't help but smile. She was glad Lily had suggested the Christmas market and delighted that she'd managed to get her husband to take time off to join her. Ruben worked hard to keep his club at the top, and Rosie was proud of him and his accomplishments.

They did get time to themselves, but not usually

around the holidays because Kenza was always jam-packed—more so than usual. During the holidays, everyone was needed, and no one, not even the boss, took time off. So, she was delighted when he agreed to bring her to the market. The open-air market was magical, with small snowflakes drifting down around them and sparkling lights adorning each stall. Their breath fogged in the crisp air, but Rosie felt warm as she snuggled into her husband's arms while they walked around. They stopped to watch carolers singing "Silent Night" while Ruben wrapped his arms around her.

She loved this time of year and wanted Ruben to enjoy it as much as she did. He grinned and hummed along to the song in her ear, so he was getting there. As "Silent Night" came to an end and the singers appeared to be taking a break, Ruben kept one arm around Rosie's shoulders and led her toward the ice rink.

Rosie knew he dreaded the ice, and she felt regretful that she had to force him to do this, since he was only doing it for her. Once they had their skates on and he still didn't want to step on the ice, she'd let him off the hook. She loved him and certainly didn't want to force him to ice skate if he didn't want to.

The rink had a large Christmas tree on one side, and Santa, reindeer, and snowmen were set up in a display that would delight anyone with a childlike spirit—herself included.

"Mmm." Rosie sighed and looked up at her husband. Her heart melted when she saw his love for her on his face. His eyes heated as she caressed his cheek. "I love you," she whispered. "I just needed to tell you."

Ruben rested his forehead against hers. "You tell me all the time, and it never gets old hearing it because I love you, too. Always, Rosie."

She reached up and kissed his cold lips, her hand against his jaw. "Will you take me on the ice?"

He grinned and answered, "I'll take you anywhere." He kissed her on the nose. "But I think we'd get arrested."

It took her a minute, but when she realized what she had said, she batted his hands away. "I can't believe you! I'm trying to be loving and romantic, and you're teasing me." She laughed.

Ruben's face fell at her words, but he grabbed her wrists and pulled her back into him. "I'm sorry." He cupped her cold face with his gloved hands. "I love you. Yes, I'll put on ice skates and hold your hand on the ice."

She smiled, fresh snowflakes landing on her lashes. "Thank you." She quickly kissed his lips before offering, "If you really don't want to go on the ice, it's okay, Ruben. I don't want to force you, and I know you'd rather watch ice hockey than be on the ice."

"Babe, I'll do anything you want. Anything for my Rosie." He kissed her cold lips gently, took her hand, and headed toward the booth for the skates.

Speechless, she let him guide her. He had her boots off and skates on before she came back to her senses. She watched her husband in silence as he sat on the bench beside her to put on his own skates. Before he could move, Rosie straddled him, wrapped her arms around his neck, and hugged him close.

Ruben tipped her face up to his. "What's wrong, Rosie?"

She shook her head and stayed silent. If she tried to talk, she'd probably burst into tears. "I'm okay," she whispered. "Just overwhelmed."

It took her a few minutes to pull herself together. She climbed shakily to her feet. She swayed on her skates, but she quickly found her balance. "Let's go on the ice." She held out her hand to Ruben, who took it as they made their way to the rink.

The rink wasn't designed for hockey matches, but rather for families to enjoy skating and for lovers to skate together. It wasn't huge, but it was big enough for their town. They spent a few minutes watching some children skate while their parents watched from the sidelines. The kids were good—much better than she and Ruben would be.

But what are a few Christmas bumps? "This looks like fun," she commented, wondering if she had made a mistake because she couldn't ice skate either. She just liked the idea of holding Ruben's hand while skating.

"Um, Rosie?"

She glanced at her husband, who grinned now that he was on to her. "You can do this, right?"

"Of course I can."

Ruben started laughing. "Come on. Just once around the rink," he said, taking her hand. "Then we can get hot chocolate with marshmallows."

"Mmm, that sounds good."

Ruben kept her steady on the ice. It turned out that she had worse balance than her husband. He managed to keep them upright...at least until they were nearing the exit. As they approached safety, Rosie breathed for the first time since being on the ice. Suddenly, a child, about eight or nine, zoomed past, sending Ruben crashing to the ice. Rosie landed on top of him. A whoosh left his lips.

They lay in a sprawl of arms and legs for a few seconds before Rosie started to laugh, followed by Ruben. "Are you okay?" Rosie giggled. "I'm sorry." She smirked. "I shouldn't laugh." She giggled again and scrambled to her feet, slipping as she climbed up the side of the rink wall. "Give me your hand, and I'll pull you up."

"No way. I'll pull you back down." Ruben rolled to his hands and knees and pulled himself up.

Rosie pulled him to her and wrapped her arms around his waist. "Thank you for doing that. I'm ready for hot chocolate now."

He hugged her before helping her off the ice.

RUBEN WAS FRUSTRATED as he sorted bills to be paid from those already paid in his office. He was usually organized, but his beautiful wife had a way of distracting him.

They'd enjoyed a warm bath together to soothe their sore muscles after ice skating at the Christmas market, which of course took longer than it should have. Hopefully, that would put an end to ice skating, and Rosie wouldn't get that idea again. He hoped she'd learned her lesson.

She challenged him in ways he loved. Her body challenged him in other ways.

In fact, her curvy body kept him semi-aroused while she was busy. He liked the mistletoe part of the holidays because, once it was up, he made sure to constantly be caught beneath it with her. She had the last laugh, though, when she pulled him close and locked lips with him. Unlike the other chaste kisses they'd exchanged under the mistletoe, this one blew his socks off and left him hard and aching. His sexy wife knew what she had done to him and continued to tease him for the rest of the day. That was probably why he was still hard and distracted behind his zipper.

Just as he was about to give up and go in search of Rosie, he heard the door handle start to turn. He sighed in relief when Rosie slipped inside. She turned the key in the lock behind her and slipped the two deadbolts home.

Knowing they were locked in his office together and seeing his wife's short dress made his balls ache. He knew that her fantasy—and his—was about to come true. From the moment she told him what she wanted, he couldn't stop thinking about it. Since they'd been together, Rosie had gotten past her shyness, learning to trust him in the process. He had never let her down, and he never would.

Rosie leaned back against the locked door. "Evening, husband."

He grinned. "Evening, wife."

ROSIE CONTINUED to hold Ruben's gaze, but made no move toward him. Instead, she leaned against the locked door, feeling her heart beat frantically in her chest with a nervous kind of excitement. Ruben made her feel alive, and she knew he loved her and her alone. This gave her the confidence she needed to carry out her fantasies and his.

She licked her lips and watched as Ruben's eyes dropped to follow her movement. "Take your clothes off. I want to see you naked."

His eyes darkened with lust at her words, and she heard his boots drop from his feet beneath the desk. He quickly removed the rest of his clothes and sat on the edge of his desk.

The throb between her thighs grew in intensity at the sight before her. Her husband was sun-kissed, and his muscles were in all the right places. She loved the hair on his chest because it would tickle and arouse her when they were close. The hair trailed down to his groin, surrounding his swollen cock, which reached up to his navel. The tip glistened with precum.

"You have too many clothes on."

She agreed and lifted her dress over her head. It dropped to the floor with a flick of her wrist, forgotten.

RUBEN DIDN'T KNOW how he was going to keep his hands off her, especially after she took off her dress and he caught a glimpse of her thigh highs. His dick jumped with excitement, craving to be inside her. He wrapped his hand around it and stroked it a few times, knowing Rosie loved to watch.

"Chair," she croaked, then cleared her throat.

Unsteady on his legs, he moved to drop his ass onto the chair. He sat and waited with his legs spread when he saw the silk ties in her hand.

She walked closer in her high heels and straddled his thighs. Her breasts were nearly at eye level. As she bent slightly to tie one of his wrists to the back of the chair, he caught a nipple in his mouth and sucked hard. Her body shuddered and her pussy rubbed against him. It took a great deal of strength not to impale her.

Rosie quickly fastened his other wrist to the chair. She put both her hands on his shoulders and held on while she used her wet pussy to rub back and forth against his rigid length. He was so hard that the veins popped, and his dick tingled and dripped with precum. He couldn't stop. Her breasts rubbed against his face. He could hardly catch his breath, his senses were on overload.

"You're killing me," he moaned.

Rosie tipped his head back and smiled down at him. "I love you." She kissed her way from his lips to his neck, chest, and abs. When she reached his navel, she dropped to her knees and kissed the crown of his penis.

Rosie teased him with a silk tie. It trailed over him like a caress, causing him to arch up. His cock was on fire and pulsed with a life of its own. But she hadn't finished teasing him. She tickled her way down his legs to his ankles, where she tied them to the chair legs.

He could easily get out of the ties if he wanted to, but being tied down while she had her way with him drove him nuts.

"You look so...aroused," she smiled, sitting back on her heels. "I don't know where to touch you first."

He didn't miss the glint of amusement that flashed in her eyes. She knew where he wanted her touch; she'd leave that spot for last. He could either growl in frustration or beg; she could take her pick.

"You know what I want," he said.

"Hmmm, and for once, I think you're going to get your wish because I'm so wet, and the need to taste you is making me throb."

Rosie let out a tortured moan that turned into a gasp when she reached out and massaged his balls. Her fingers spread and rubbed between his legs while his cock pulsed, close to release. When he started to pant, she released him and smirked.

"As much as I love watching your release leave your body, I want to ride you."

"Fuck, Rosie. I want this so badly, but damn it, you have me close. And I mean close."

"Hmm."

She tickled her way up from his feet, tracing his trembling thighs with her hands, and finally gripped his shaft. Her head dipped as he braced himself for the feel of her mouth. He hadn't lied about being close; he was afraid he wouldn't be able to control the urge to climax.

"Gentle," he hissed and groaned when her tongue licked and swirled around the sensitive head. "Hard, and I'll come." She took him into the warm recesses of her mouth, and he couldn't control his hips, which thrust up at the sensation. His movement was limited by the silk ties, which he would soon rip free.

ROSIE LOVED HAVING Ruben's cock in her mouth. Although he was aroused and hard, he was smooth except for the pulsing vein. As she pulled back to the tip and swirled her tongue around to catch the precum trickling out of his slit, she moaned.

She knew her husband loved being restrained because it heightened his pleasure, a discovery they had made together. He'd spent most of his life doing the restraining, but with her, it had worked both ways for a while.

Once Ruben started grinding into her mouth, she knew it was time to finish him off, but only if she rode him. With one last suck, she let him slip from her mouth, then licked her way up his torso.

Back on her feet, she straddled him and lowered herself onto his cock. Her mouth hovered over Ruben's, and their gasps of pleasure were locked between them.

His hands were finally free and he gripped her hips. "I need you to move," he growled and started rocking her on his cock. She was so wet and swollen that her pussy gripped his cock, trying to hold on when he pulled back. He was stronger, though. As his mouth tugged on a nipple, she rippled and convulsed over him. He started to shoot his release inside her. The strong pulls of her vagina milked more out of him and caused his penis to twitch and release until they were both exhausted.

"Fuck, babe," he finally gasped. "I seriously didn't think I'd last long enough to get inside you."

"I didn't think you would either." She slipped her arms around his neck and held him tightly. "I love you," she whispered. "So much."

He gulped a few times as she watched him become overwhelmed with emotion. She knew how much he loved her. Until she'd come into his life, he hadn't been looking for love. Now, he had it forever. They both did.

"RUBEN, LOOK OUTSIDE!" Rosie shouted, her voice sharp with excitement.

He knew it had obviously been snowing hard because his wife was obsessed with snow. Just an inch of the white stuff and she instantly became a child again. She loved being outdoors in it. He liked it at first, but after freezing his ass off for a few weeks, de-icing the cars, and clearing the sidewalk around Kenza, he was ready to be done with it.

His wife made him enjoy it again.

As a child, he lived outdoors no matter the season, as did his brothers. They got into trouble on occasion, but he wouldn't trade his memories of that time for anything.

"Ruben, did you look?" Rosie bounced into the bedroom where he'd just finished getting dressed.

He chuckled and caught her in his arms. "Not yet," he answered, bending down to capture her lips. "I take it there's more snow on the ground?" He raised an eyebrow.

"And then some."

He groaned. A heavy snowstorm hadn't been forecasted, but then again, he'd been preoccupied with his sexy wife last night.

"I think you need to stay home and cuddle up with me. I'll make us some hot chocolate." She smiled.

He didn't want to refuse such a tempting offer, but he had to finish her Christmas present. He just didn't know how to refuse her without lying. The last thing he wanted was to tell her what he was doing. He decided he could tell her a partial truth. "I can't, babe. I haven't had breakfast yet, and your offer is tempting, but I have to pick up your present today."

"Present?" Her eyes sparkled with pleasure.

He laughed. "Yes." He kissed her quickly. "Before you get the wrong idea, I've already stashed some things away that you won't be able to find." He knew she would start rooting around as soon as he left. "But I had to order the last thing." That was a bit of a stretch, but he didn't want her to think he'd forgotten; the present he was finalizing had been in the works for about six weeks. He only hoped he could wait until Christmas Eve to give her the gift.

LUCIEN & SABRINA

LUCIEN SAT in the dark of his bedroom and watched his wife and son sleep. He still couldn't believe that he was married and had a son who would be three months old soon, Alexander.

Before he was scarred, he wanted a woman of his own, but he never thought it would be possible. Sabrina had other ideas, though. He smiled, remembering their encounters before he finally slept with her. Just one taste, and he was in trouble. No matter how much he pushed her away, she came back to him until the last time he went to her.

They had made a home in Colorado, but he missed his family, and he knew both of Alexander's grandmothers missed them and their new grandson. He'd thought a lot about it during the past month that they'd been back. He hadn't mentioned anything to Sabrina, but he was almost certain that he wanted to move back to Lexington. They both loved their house, but he could find them something similar near his family. He was sure of it. If he couldn't find something similar, he would build it.

He was tired of thinking about it. He was tired of watching over his family at night the way he had been. Sabrina had no idea that he spent most nights watching them sleep. She'd be upset if she knew. She knew something was wrong because he couldn't hide his fatigue from her. He had yet to admit his fear that one day he would wake up and realize it had all been a dream. He knew that would kill him.

His wife hadn't missed anything, though, and she'd soon call him out on it. He watched her roll over in the large bed they shared and search for him in her sleep. Of course, she came up empty. "Lucien?" she whispered, her voice husky with sleep.

He quickly stood up, climbed back into bed, and pulled her into his arms. "I'm right here." It's early. Go back to sleep." He kissed her forehead, held her, and soon fell back asleep.

SABRINA KNEW that something was bothering her husband. She had caught him watching them while they slept. She'd always pretended to be asleep until that morning, but she couldn't watch him do that anymore. She didn't doubt his love for her or Alexander, and she hoped he didn't doubt hers for them.

He was a wonderful father and husband who only settled down when she was in the room with him. It was as though he was afraid she'd disappear. She had no intention of doing that.

She wanted to talk to him about it, but she wasn't sure if he was ready for her questions or if she was ready for his answers. All she knew was that he had to stop, as the fatigue was evident on his face.

He sat at the kitchen table reading papers from work, trying to stifle a yawn behind his coffee mug. He was exhausted, and his exhaustion was affecting him in more ways than one. It was time for them to talk.

Sabrina quickly checked that their son was still asleep in the breakfast room, then went back to her husband, making room for herself on his lap.

He smiled and set his paper and coffee down on

the table. "Mmm," he said, nuzzling her neck. Goose bumps broke out over her skin at the sensual touch. "You taste good." He licked and nibbled his way down her neck.

Sabrina ran her fingers through his hair, pushing his head back so she could look into his eyes. She cupped his face in her hands and pulled him close to meet her lips.

Since things had been resolved between them, Lucien had gradually become more relaxed around Sabrina regarding his scars. She knew it hadn't been easy for him, but she'd shown him through her care and love that she loved everything about him, including the damage to his skin.

Their foreheads rested together as their gazes met and held. Sabrina couldn't hold her concern inside any longer, so she asked, "Will you talk to me? I know you sit up and watch Alexander and me sleep. It's like you're protecting us or making sure we don't disappear on you. But I need to know what's going on because I'm worried about you."

She knew her husband could see the worry on her face and hear it in her voice. He should have known that she'd be on to him. She didn't miss a damn thing.

"I'm fine." He brushed the hair back from her face. "I'll always be fine as long as I have you."

His words told her all she needed to know.

She turned and straddled him, wrapping her arms around his neck. She whispered, "I love you. You have my heart, Lucien. Without you in my life, I'd be so broken that no one could ever put me back together. Are you hearing me?" Tears brimmed in her eyes before slowly falling down her cheeks.

Lucien held her tightly against him. "I'm listening," he began, but he had to stop to catch his breath. "Since Alexander was born, I've struggled to sleep," he admitted. "You two are my world. I'm afraid that one morning I'll wake up and realize it was all just a dream."

She sat up and cupped his face in her hands. "It isn't a dream. We're here with you forever. Please don't suffer alone. Talk to me about how you're feeling. I know you're a guy, macho and all that," she smiled, "but I'm your wife. You can tell me anything. It hurts when you keep things from me."

"I'm sorry. I thought it would go away."

"And it hasn't, right?"

Lucien shook his head. "No."

"Do you think it all stems from what happened to you?"

"It's all connected." He stroked her cheek and rubbed her lips with his thumb. "I love you." He kissed her quickly, still holding her in his arms. "Unless you untangle your legs from around my waist, I'm going to get busy on the kitchen table."

She knew he was trying to lighten the mood, and she let him. They'd talked, and although she was still worried about him, she was glad she knew what the problem was. Maybe he suffered from anxiety or something similar. She'd keep an eye on him, and she knew he knew it. Her husband's life had been turned upside down when they met, and even more so when she found out she was pregnant. Maybe he just needed to see how she felt.

He groaned. "Oh, no. We're not going to have sex on the kitchen table with our son over there."

Sabrina wiggled against him. He was certainly up for it. "You sure about that?"

"Hmm, for now." He untangled himself, pulled her into his arms for a kiss, and then went to retrieve their squirming son, who had woken up.

THE SUN WAS SETTING as he walked along the sidewalk, holding his beautiful wife's hand. Their son had been left at home under the watchful eye of his uncle, Dante, who was Lucien's cousin. Lucien felt better after talking with Sabrina and was surprised she hadn't told him to stop being an idiot.

He should have known better. She'd never tell him that, and she took his worries seriously. He'd spent many years after the fire feeling the way he did now. Even though he didn't want to admit it, he knew the anxiety had returned. With Sabrina by his side, he could survive anything, so he had no qualms about talking to her about it anymore—like he should have done from the beginning—just not while they were shopping for gifts.

"We need to go in here," Sabrina said as they passed a store.

He had only a chance for a quick glance at the sign before she dragged him inside.

Victoria's Secret.

What was it with the women in his family? He'd spoken to Sebastian the day before, who had gone on and on about his trip to the store and the feel of lace against his fingers. He'd actually only half listened because, while Sebastian rambled about silk and the feel of the lace against his fingers, Sabrina had been on her hands and knees in front of him, playing with their son, who was on a play mat. Lucien was abrupt with his brother because he felt guilty for having lustful thoughts while she was with their son.

"Earth to Lucien." Sabrina broke into his thoughts.

He grinned at her and pulled her closer. "I was thinking about you bending over for me."

Her eyes widened before she smacked his arm.

"Ouch! What was that for?"

"We're in public." She snickered. "Remember when it was close to my due date and I was always horny?"

"How could I forget?" He chuckled.

"You seriously turned me on at that restaurant, and I dragged you into the disabled restroom."

He groaned. "Woman! Did you have to bring that up in here, surrounded by all these lacy panties?"

Her face lit up as she realized what she was doing to him. "Hmmm, I bet there's something else up."

Shaking his head at her teasing, he reached for the scrap of lace closest to him. It turned out to be a black thong priced at over two hundred dollars. Who would pay that much for a thong?

"I prefer this," Sabrina said, holding up a different thong.

Lucien turned, and when he spotted what she held, his eyes froze. In fact, his whole body froze. She held a transparent purple babydoll set out in front of her. His heart rate picked up, and his cock twitched in his pants.

"Fuck," he hissed.

Sabrina knew damn well what she was doing to him, but he snapped, "You need to try that on and something else." He grabbed his wife and a sweat suit set with one hand as they passed the display and headed for the changing rooms.

As luck would have it, the changing rooms were unattended, so he quickly dragged her to the back and inside an empty cubicle.

"Lucien, I'm not..."

He slammed his lips down, sealing her words in her throat. Her talk in the store and the hot memory had made him horny as fuck. His dick was so hard it hurt, squished in his underwear like that.

"Try it on," he begged in a whisper. He sure as hell didn't want anyone to find them in there together.

Lucien stood to one side with his eyes closed,

listening to the rustling of material as his wife changed clothes. It took him only seconds before he opened his eyes again and watched her pull the babydoll over her nude body.

Before she finished, he had undone his pants, taken out his swollen cock, and gripped it in his hand. His arousal heightened with the sight of Sabrina and his own touch as he stroked his flesh. They were about to have the quickest fuck in history. As Sabrina straightened and saw him, her eyes widened, then darkened with lust.

He pounced. "God, you're so fucking sexy. I'm seconds from coming."

"I'm ready, Lucien." She met his gaze. "Make me come," she whispered.

He lifted her into his arms and thrust into her. Their groans were muffled as their mouths met. Lucien held her against the wall with his hips and stomach while his hands roamed over the top of her babydoll to pinch and roll her nipples. They leaked milk, and he knew they were sensitive to the touch.

He backed up, dropped into the chair in the corner, and nearly came when Sabrina took all of him inside her. He bottomed out and couldn't catch his breath. Sabrina ground down on him as her vaginal walls rippled along his length. That was all it took for him to follow her over the edge. He quickly shoved the material up her torso, sucked an engorged nipple, and felt the pull inside her as tremors of pleasure ran through her.

She tried to push his head away, but he just switched breasts. The milk for their child tasted horrible, but knowing how sensitive her nipples were, he couldn't resist sucking on them.

"Oh, God," she whispered. "I'm going to come again if you don't stop."

"Come on my dick, babe."

He continued sucking her nipple while his other hand found her sensitive clit. He stimulated her until he was hard and aching inside her, and then she flooded him. Her pleasure was caught in his mouth so that they wouldn't be discovered.

His dick was rock-solid, but he knew they couldn't stay in the changing rooms any longer. He should have known better than to start something with her when they couldn't spend all day together. Instead of shopping, they should have checked into a hotel. They made love often at home, but not as leisurely as they once did, since they had to schedule it around the baby's naps.

"We better get dressed," Sabrina suggested, but she didn't move to do so. "But, um, you're still hard."

"I'm always hard when I think of you or when you're in front of me."

SABRINA STOOD ON UNSTEADY LEGS, quickly took off the babydoll, and put her own clothes back on while watching her husband. He hadn't zipped himself back up yet, though his eyes were closed and his head was thrown back. She knew he was trying to regain control, but she had a better idea.

She dropped to her knees between his thighs. Lucien didn't have time to protest before her mouth was on him. She smiled around his shaft when she felt his legs tremble and his hand slide into her hair.

She dipped her hand between his thighs to play with his testicles as she sucked him deep. His girth was wide, but she managed to take half of him inside, swirling her tongue around the crown as she did so. His essence dripped from the slit, which she lapped up without hesitation.

She had discovered early on in their relationship that her husband had a sensitive spot on his dick. The slightest pressure would cause him to explode. It was on the part that had burned slightly, so to make sure she wouldn't hurt him, she always ran her fingers over that spot first. He always gave it away because his breathing changed when she touched the spot. She held him tightly in her mouth, sucking when she pressed his button, hearing his breath catch in his throat as he came.

She met his gaze as his release filled her mouth, and she swallowed it all. She let him see her love, smiling around him when he returned the sentiment.

Bang… Bang… Bang.

The banging on the door made Sabrina jump up and straighten her clothes. Lucien was more laid back. He took his time putting his dick away, the smile of pleasure still plastered on his face.

"Anyone inside?"

"Yeah," Sabrina replied.

"Just a minute," Lucien said.

There was a pause, and then they heard, "Not again," as the store assistant moved away.

Sabrina snickered, wondering how many couples had done what they had just done.

❄

AS LUCIEN WATCHED his mom cradle Alexander, he made his decision. His mom and Sabrina, who sat beside her, both had tears in their eyes. His wife met his gaze, and he hoped she was telling him without words that she wanted to move back to Lexington. They hadn't discussed it, but he knew it was time to put the cards on the table.

"Hello, son," his father greeted him as he walked over to peek at his grandson. "How are things?" He kissed Sabrina on the head and walked over to him.

His father wrapped him in a hug. "It's good to have you home."

He felt an ache in his chest at his father's words. "It's good to be home. We're all doing well."

"I'm glad to hear that." Elias took a seat next to his wife. He'd probably realized that it was the only way he was going to see his grandson, at least for now. "Come and sit with us. You look as though you're about to run out the door."

His father wasn't too far off the mark. Elias had considered finding a quiet place to think and get his emotions under control. With the way he felt, anyone would think that he was the one who'd had the baby instead of Sabrina. He loved his family, and now that he no longer felt the need to hide, he wanted to come home. He'd need to talk to his dad about the idea forming in his mind. Instead of house hunting, he thought Sabrina might like to design their own home on the land gifted to him by his parents. He didn't see why they would say no, since Michael, Ramon, and Sebastian had all built their homes on their section of the land. The more he thought about it, the more he couldn't stop.

"Are you okay?" Sabrina's soft hand slipped around his scarred one. The worry in her voice was clear.

He frowned.

"You spaced out."

"Shit. Sorry." He grinned and pulled her onto his lap. "I'm fine."

She didn't believe him, and he didn't blame her, given how he'd been acting lately.

"I promise." He kissed her nose. "We'll talk later," he whispered. "But I promise it's nothing awful."

"I'm still going to worry until you tell me what's going on with you."

He didn't want that, so he went for it. "How would you feel about moving back to Lexington?"

"Permanently?"

"I think so."

"Yes." She kissed his lips. "Yes." She kissed his nose. "Yes." She kissed his lips again. "Oh, God, Please don't tell me this is a joke."

He laughed. "No joke." He caressed her face. "I think it's what we need to do. We need our families around us just as much as they need us around them."

When he finished talking, they glanced at his parents, who both had their heads dipped toward their grandson. He watched his grandparents with fascination.

"We'll talk more about it later, but right now, I'm going to head into the kitchen and make the coffee Mom offered." Lucien stood and left his wife with his parents.

SABRINA WATCHED her husband leave the room. Then she sat next to his mother and watched her in-laws cuddle and coo at her son. She knew what Lucien had suggested had to happen. She was happy in Denver, but she'd be happier in Lexington with her family around.

"Sabrina, we're ignoring you. I'm sorry," Pippa said. Pippa leaned closer and took her hand. "I'm just overwhelmed to have Lucien's son in my arms. It's still hard to believe that he has everything he ever wanted but didn't expect." Tears gathered on Pippa's lashes. "He's happy, isn't he?"

"I'm happy, Mom," Lucien answered as he carried in a tray of refreshments.

"That was quick," Sabrina said.

"Mom had already put the tray out, and the coffee had finished brewing." Lucien smiled and set everything down on the coffee table. He clasped his mom's and Sabrina's hands and looked at his mom. "Please stop worrying about me, Mom. Sabrina and our son make me happy."

Pippa passed Alexander to his grandfather and sniffled into a tissue. "I'm glad."

While his mom poured the coffee, Lucien moved to snuggle with his wife on the sofa. Nothing had ever felt as right as having Sabrina in his arms. She had no problem showing her affection for him in public, and he loved that. He'd never been one to draw attention to himself, but he loved how she would glow, especially since he was the reason why.

A noise at the front door drew their attention. He

grinned when his brother, Ramon, walked inside with his fiancé, Noah. Their wedding was arranged for New Year's Day at their parents' ranch house, now that gay marriage had been legalized in Kentucky.

When he embraced his brother, he said, "It's good to see you." Lucien had hidden his emotions behind a wall, but Sabrina had knocked them down. He hadn't admitted to himself that he needed his family until then, which was probably why the hug between brothers lasted longer than usual.

"You okay?" Ramon frowned.

Lucien grinned. "I've never been better."

Ramon looked doubtful.

"Seriously." Lucien lightly punched his brother in the shoulder before greeting Noah.

Noah introduced his brother to Lucien. Although it felt strange at first, Lucien accepted that his brother was with a man without a problem. He loved his youngest brother, and they'd all been raised to accept everyone, so he felt just as comfortable with Ramon being with a man as he would have if he were with a woman.

"So, how are the wedding arrangements going?" Sabrina asked after sitting back down.

Noah laughed, and Ramon turned and frowned at him. "It's going," he commented.

"What he means is," Noah added, "the caterer is being a pain in the ass. One minute she has everything settled; the next, she's on the phone again, wanting to change something. I'm convinced she has a crush on Ramon." Noah shook his head. "It would be annoying if it weren't so entertaining."

"At my expense," Ramon mumbled, sounding unhappy.

"Now, stop, you two. Your wedding is in ten days; I don't want any disagreements." Their mom absent-mindedly caressed Alexander's cheek, her eyes filling with tears. "All I want is for my youngest baby to be happy."

Lucien snickered at the horror on Ramon's face. It was nice not being in the hot seat with his mom for a change. Usually, she was on his case.

He leaned back and pulled Sabrina into his arms as he watched his brother react to their mom.

"Mom," Ramon groaned. "Please, don't start with the tears."

"You're my son. Why wouldn't I be emotional about you getting married? You're my last baby to leave the nest."

Ramon groaned. "I haven't lived at home for years, and I'm not that far away. Five minutes down the lane isn't bad."

"You know exactly what I mean, so stop."

Ramon got up from his seat and kissed their mom on the top of her head.

5

CHRISTMAS EVE

LILY HUMMED to herself in the kitchen, feeling excited. Michael had finished bathing the children, which surprised her. He usually helped with bath time, but he insisted that she deserved a night off and that he could handle it on his own. Still, she listened out for a shout for help while she made hot chocolate for her two oldest children. She made herself and Michael some, too, because she wanted to start a Christmas tradition for their family.

The items the children were going to leave for Santa were spread out on the kitchen table so they could make their own Santa plates and avoid squabbling. She was taking apple pies and applesauce to her in-laws the following day, so she put them in the utility room to keep them cool. Lily was delighted when Pippa agreed to let her daughters-in-law help with the Christmas meal.

Pippa loved doing everything herself and was like a one-woman army, but Lily and Carla had explained that they felt useless if they didn't do something, too. Pippa finally agreed, and they each picked something to do. When Lily mentioned it to Rosie and Sabrina, they also insisted on making something.

Michael was the first to give in, and Lily enjoyed watching his brothers chase their tails. Lily loved her sisters-in-law and always looked forward to Sabrina being back in town. Sabrina had been Lily's best friend for years before Lily met Michael. She no longer felt lonely or as if something was missing. Michael and their children filled the void that had plagued her life until she met him and his family. Now, they completed everything else.

But now, as she heard "Jingle Bells" being sung downstairs, she smiled and pressed a hand to her chest in delight. The singing grew louder, and then they appeared in the kitchen doorway.

Charlotte started to giggle, and her brother Michael Jr. gave her a friendly shove before falling over laughing himself. They looked so cute in their elf pajamas, and Sirena matched them in her elf romper. Michael wore a Santa hat and a beautiful grin. His eyes lit up when they settled on her.

She walked over to him and curved her hand around his neck, bringing him down to meet her lips. Her husband never had a problem with that. He slipped a hand around her waist and pulled her closer as he bent his head to meet her lips.

The noise of their children caused him to pull back slightly. With a smile filled with love, he gave her a quick kiss before releasing her so she could go to the twins.

They both wanted to be in her arms, but she could no longer lift them both now that they were older. She distracted them by kissing each of them on the cheek before helping them into their chairs at the table.

"Make sure you only put one of each on the Santa plates, okay, guys?" She told them, pushing the plates closer to their eager hands.

Watching over them, she came back to Michael, wrapped her arm around his waist, and snuggled close. Sirena started to wiggle, so she placed a hand on her belly to tease their baby girl.

"You sit with the twins at the table, and I'll warm

up a bottle for her." She smiled and kissed his cheek before doing so.

MICHAEL SAT NEXT to Charlotte and smiled as she drank her chocolate milk.

Three years ago, he never would have guessed that his future would hold a beautiful wife and three children. He and Lily both wanted a large family, but he'd be happy if they stopped at three. He hated seeing Lily so uncomfortable with her huge, swollen belly. Still, knowing she carried his child was the biggest turn-on. Lily never complained and always said it would be worth it in the end. He had to agree; it was worth it. He just hated the worry that came with it. When she was in labor, his wife complained that his job was easy compared to hers: all he had to do was get his rocks off. She certainly had the maternity staff amused and apologized to him when she remembered what she said.

He loved her, and who knew what the future held? For now, he had a wiggling baby in his arms and a bottle of warm milk to feed her.

Sirena fed quickly and fell asleep in his arms. He

laid her down in her bassinet in the living room and joined his wife and twins on the sofa. Lily produced a book that she wanted to be one of the family stories for a few years, until the children were old enough to sit through The Little Match Girl.

AFTER FINISHING the fire in the hearth, Sebastian turned to find his wife comfortably seated on the sofa. She was wearing a pair of his thick socks and smiled softly when his lingering gaze finally landed on her face.

His love for her grew stronger every day, and he couldn't imagine life without her. She made him feel whole and made him long for the family growing inside her.

"Come sit with me," she said. Carla held out her hand to him. He didn't hesitate to take it and sit down beside her.

He wrapped his arm around her shoulders, pulling her against his chest.

They laughed when Buttons jumped onto the sofa —or rather, tried to. She fell back to the floor, so Carla moved to pick up the mewling animal before settling back down. The cat started to purr and settled in the curve of Carla's neck, but on his chest. Buttons looked so cute curled up asleep that it was hard not to pet her.

"Isn't she sweet?" Carla wanted him to agree and chuckled when he grunted. "Don't listen to him, Buttons. He's a big softy."

He listened to his wife as she continued talking to the cat and smiled. She was crazy, but he loved her. And yeah, he liked the cat. The cat was cute, but he didn't want his wife to know that.

The logs crackled in the hearth, and he realized that he had never felt more content. He had the woman he loved in his arms, and a baby was on the way. He tried to keep his overactive libido in check because it was Christmas Eve, and he wanted to sit quietly and think. He wasn't sure what he wanted to think about, but the coziness was nice.

Then his wife stroked his belly, and his good intentions started to go out the window as his dick swelled with arousal behind his zipper.

Carla snickered and placed her hand on top of it. "Sorry, I just wanted to see how easily I could arouse you."

Was she serious?

"Babe, I only have to look at you, and I'm hard as fuck. Tonight, I was trying to behave while we sat in front of the fire." He took her hand and put it on his chest, next to the kitten.

"We'll have plenty of other Christmas Eves where we'll have to behave." She purred against him. "This is our last Christmas Eve with just the two of us. Next year, we'll be celebrating with our son or daughter." Carla placed her hand on her stomach. "I can't believe there's a tiny life growing inside me."

She was right. He'd be a daddy by next Christmas Eve, and Carla would be a mommy. Their lives would change for the better. He would really have to curb his sexual appetite for his wife when the baby arrived, but he wasn't a teenager. He'd manage.

"I think I need to keep you naked from now until you give birth so I can get rid of all my sexual desire."

Carla snickered. "Having constant sex for the next seven months won't get rid of your sexual desire. I can guarantee that."

"I think we should try." He struggled to keep a straight face.

"Hmm," Carla said, glancing away, and he frowned.

One minute she was teasing him, and the next she

was serious. "Babe, what's wrong?" He brushed the hair behind her ear and cupped her jaw.

When she didn't answer or look at him, he tilted her head back to look at her. "Carla, you have me worried." He met her gaze, along with the tears hovering on her lashes.

He put the kitten on the blanket next to him and turned fully to face his wife.

"What if you don't like me when I have a big belly? You might not want to make love to me then."

His eyes popped wide. "Oh God, Carla. I love you. There's no way I won't ever want to make love to you. You keep me constantly horny." He cupped her face. "I can't wait to see you swollen with our child, knowing that it's me who got you that way." He grinned. "Don't for one minute think that I won't want you." He kissed her then.

Every word he said was true. He loved her and couldn't wait to see their child growing inside her. Then he remembered reading something: "Besides," he added, "pregnancy hormones can apparently make you horny. More so than usual." He raised his eyebrows, trying to lighten the mood.

CARLA CHUCKLED AT HER HUSBAND. She knew he loved her, couldn't keep his hands off her, and that it would never change. She had just been caught off guard by the news that she was pregnant, as it hadn't been planned. She was happy and looking forward to being a mom to her little one; she just hadn't expected it for a few more years. In fact, she was surprised that she hadn't gotten pregnant sooner, given how her husband couldn't leave her alone. She couldn't complain, though, because she was just as bad. Quite often, she'd dress to tease him, knowing he wouldn't be able to ignore her.

"Sebastian, I think you should give me one of those Victoria's Secret packages early so you can see what it looks like. I mean, we won't have time for a fashion show tomorrow morning."

Her husband groaned. "I'm not sure seeing you in hardly anything is going to help me have a quiet night by the fire."

She grinned and rolled her eyes. "It'll still be a quiet night by the fire. It'll be slow," she breathed against his mouth. "Long and slow." She placed her hand in his lap and smiled when she felt him harden against her.

"You make it hard for me to refuse."

They both chuckled at his choice of words.

Carla loved the feel of her husband's naked body, which was why she couldn't wait. She quickly unfastened his jeans. She sighed with pleasure when his cock was freed and in her hand, and he captured her sigh in his mouth.

"I love you, Sebastian. Tonight, I'm going to show you how much."

ON CHRISTMAS EVE, Ruben felt like a child about to open his presents: he was eager and excited. He had done so well, keeping Rosie completely in the dark about what he had been up to. He only hoped it would stay that way a little while longer.

While he cleaned the snow from his truck, Rosie was inside doing some last-minute wrapping. She'd already wrapped the staff's presents and left them in the staff room for after their shift ended. Rosie was under the impression that he was finished with her presents. She'd soon find out that he hadn't.

They'd both had enough of living above Kenza. Although Rosie never complained and told him constantly that she was happy wherever he was, it was time to move out. That, of course, was where his surprise came in.

"What are you doing?"

Ruben whipped his head around at Rosie's surprised question. She stood silhouetted in the doorway, wearing boots and a winter jacket.

"I'm clearing the truck so we can go out." He hid his smile as he knocked the packed snow off the back wheels.

"Out? It's Christmas Eve."

"I know, and that's why we're going out." Ruben stopped and grinned at his beautiful wife. "I want to show you your Christmas present." He walked closer and stood a mere foot away.

Rosie raised her eyebrows and laughed. Her eyes glanced at his crotch. She liked this kind of present.

"You'll get that present much later. For now, you need to get in the truck so I can drive you there."

He could tell by the way her eyes lit up that she was excited. However, it was clear that she didn't want to show just how excited she was. He grinned, excitement running through him, and stayed silent.

He helped her into the cab of his truck and smiled to himself as he joined her before pulling out from the back of the club.

Everything was closed tight for the night, and Kenza would be soon. He'd agreed to close the doors at eleven so his employees could go home to their families and friends to spend Christmas morning with them. That's one advantage of owning a business: being fair to your employees.

"How far is it?" Rosie asked.

"You'll just have to wait and see." He smirked and laughed when Rosie fidgeted in her seat with excitement.

As he turned onto the snow-covered street, Rosie perked up, glanced at him, and looked at the darkened house on the corner toward which they were heading. He pulled into the driveway without saying a word and turned the engine off.

Rosie turned to him, her mouth opening and closing silently.

He smirked and walked around to open her door. He wrapped his arms around her and under her legs and hauled her out into the snow.

Once she was on her feet, he took her hand and led her to the porch. He took the key from his pocket, unlocked the front door, and lifted his wife back into his arms. He carried her over the threshold and smiled. "Merry Christmas, baby. Welcome to our new home."

She started to cry, and he panicked.

Had he made a mistake? Did she not like the house?

He walked over to the stairs, sat down, and held Rosie in his arms. She wrapped her arms around his neck and sobbed. He couldn't speak. He didn't know what to say anyway, so he just held her tightly as his neck grew wet from her tears.

After a few minutes, Rosie pulled back and used the tissue he offered her. "You bought us a house?" She sniffled.

"I did. I thought you loved this house."

Rosie put her hand over his mouth so he couldn't say anything else.

"I love this house, and I love you. I never expected to live here, but you bought it for us." Tears threatened again. "Thank you." She started to cry again.

He hated seeing tears on her beautiful face and never knew how to calm her down. After her words, he hoped they were tears of happiness.

"Rosie, are you sure this is the house you want?"

She started to laugh. "I promise you, this is the most amazing Christmas present ever. I don't think anything will ever top this." She kissed him slowly and deeply. "When can we move in?"

"Whenever you want."

"So it's ours already, and you haven't just borrowed the key?"

What was she saying?

"Because," she said, climbing from his lap and unzipping her jacket, "I think we need to christen the stairs...now, Ruben."

He didn't need to be told twice.

WHILE LUCIEN GOT Alexander ready for bed and gave him his bedtime feeding, Sabrina put the finishing touches on their Christmas Eve dinner. She had cooked beef stew and dumplings, followed by a light chocolate mousse—Lucien's favorite.

Sabrina was still worried about her husband, but they had been in Lexington for a couple of days, and he already seemed to be in a better mood. It was as though his worry had fallen away now that he was close to his family. She didn't know how to feel about that because she was his family, too.

Her husband wasn't only layered with scars; he

had so much depth that it scared her sometimes. They'd had a very rocky start that lasted quite a while, but once he'd taken her to his house in Denver, everything fell into place. Now, however, she wasn't too sure what was going on with him. She knew what he told her, but getting anything else out of him was like getting a tooth pulled at the dentist—painful.

The meal was now on the table, and her one glass of wine for the evening was poured.

Instead of waiting for Lucien to appear, she decided to go down to their son's bedroom and watch her two men together. Her socks meant she wouldn't make a sound, and as she approached, she heard Lucien whispering to their son. She couldn't make out what he said, but she saw that he had a book on his lap. He glanced at their son in his arms, then back to the book as he read a Christmas story. Her heart melted.

Lucien glanced up and noticed her. The smile he reserved for her was radiant. At that moment, she knew there was no reason to worry. Her husband was truly happy with them, and, if she was honest with herself, they were both happier being back in Kentucky.

He stood, placed their son in his crib, and, with

one last glance, walked toward her. Seeing the look on his face, Sabrina felt as if her heart might burst. He cupped her face in his hands, tenderly caressing each cheekbone. He backed her out of the room and kissed her. He kissed her long and deep, until her knees started to buckle and her toes curled with delight.

LUCIEN HAD SEEN the look on Sabrina's face before she masked it with a smile. She'd been worried, and he knew he had caused it. If he hadn't voiced his concerns at his wife's urging, she wouldn't have had anything else to worry about.

He broke off the kiss and smiled when she moaned and tried to capture his mouth with her own. "More." She kissed his chin and moved down to his neck and collarbone.

"Let's go eat and talk because I can see the worry in your eyes."

She dropped her head to his chest, and he felt her inhale against him.

"You smell good. You always do." Sabrina smiled up at him and let him take her hand as they walked to the beautifully set table.

The table was made of black marble, and Sabrina had placed green napkins down to match the red plates. He smiled. She must have done some shopping because he only remembered having black plates in the cupboards.

"You like?" She smiled and urged him to take his seat.

She had made his favorite dish and served it with potatoes. His belly rumbled at the sight of it, but he found that he couldn't eat just yet. He needed to convince Sabrina that he was really all right. He took a sip of wine and said, "I love you."

He was glad he caught her off guard. She knew he loved her, but he didn't usually just blurt it out.

"Back in Denver, I suffered from anxiety, Sabrina. It was an accumulation of my life being turned upside down for the better. Once we arrived in Lexington and I told you about moving back here, everything seemed to fall into place."

Sabrina reached for his hand and stayed silent while he continued.

"When I locked my emotions away, I found it easier to live away from my family. But once I had you and eventually Alexander, everything was unlocked, and I missed being here." He sighed. "Am I making any sense to you?"

"Oh, Lucien. You're making so much sense, and I'm glad you've finally let the past go. That's what you're telling me, isn't it?"

He felt tearful at Sabrina's words because she was right. He had finally let the past go and was looking forward to their future in Lexington.

"Fuck," was the last word to leave Ramon's mouth before his cell shattered on the hearth. That woman was going to be the death of him.

He turned around and found Noah standing behind him, smiling widely as he tried to contain his laughter. "What did she say?" Noah finally gave in and chuckled.

"You would find it funny," Ramon grumbled.

He'd be very surprised if the wedding guests had eaten anything. The caterer was a pain in the ass. In fact, much to his embarrassment, she wanted his dick, which was why she was being so awkward.

God, give him strength.

Noah finished pouring himself a coffee and faced

his fiancé. "I find it amusing that the caterer is after you when she's supposed to be planning the meal for our wedding."

"You're not jealous? Why aren't you jealous?"

"Ramon, you're acting like a child." Noah rolled his eyes. "I'm not jealous because she isn't a threat to our relationship. No one is," he admitted.

It shut Ramon up instantly.

"You want a fight, but I refuse to give you one." Noah headed outside, dropped his jeans, and climbed into the hot tub while Ramon watched.

Noah was right, of course. Ramon had wanted to fight to release the sexual tension. They had agreed not to have sex or give each other hand jobs until after their wedding on New Year's Day, so he was extremely frustrated. Seeing Noah naked in the hot tub didn't help.

"Ramon, let it go and join me in here."

"I'm not sure that's a good idea," Ramon admitted.

"I agree, but it's Christmas Eve, and I want you in here with me."

He smiled and found that his feet were moving on their own. Before he knew it, he was standing at the side of the tub. Ramon reached out and ran his hands through Noah's hair, feeling him shudder at the touch.

"Mmm, don't tempt me. Please behave."

Ramon took a deep breath, stepped away, stripped, and joined his guy in the hot water. It was freezing outside, but the tub made up for that. So did the company.

NOAH WATCHED Ramon climb into the tub, his knuckles gripping the ledge to stop himself from reaching out. Ramon had a beautiful body, and when he was aroused, he reminded Noah of a Greek god—all muscle, with his rigid length sticking out from his body.

Ramon sat in the water while Noah closed his eyes, trying to control his body. No sex meant no sex. If only his body realized that.

Noah opened his eyes when he heard Ramon clear his throat. He glanced over and saw the smirk on Ramon's face.

Noah chuckled at having been caught thinking about Ramon's body. It was written all over his face.

"So, what the hell are we going to do about Miss. Painintheass?"

Noah couldn't help but laugh. "I have a brilliant idea."

When silence fell, Ramon grumbled, "I'm waiting to hear your wonderful idea."

"Impatient as always." Noah grinned. "You need to set your mom on her." She was disappointed that you wouldn't let her help with the arrangements because you're a control freak. I think you'd make her day if you passed it on to her."

Ramon grinned. "I've been thinking about that. She'd set her straight, and it would get her out of our hair."

"It would."

RAMON TRIED to appear relaxed while sitting in the hot tub with Noah, even though he was anything but.

He had fond memories of the hot tub, all of which involved them being naked together.

Noah smirked and moved closer between Ramon's legs. Ramon gulped and groaned when

Noah stood in front of him, naked, before climbing out of the tub.

"Glad that's sorted. I'm going to bed."

He left Ramon with his mouth hanging open, his balls aching and his dick throbbing.

"Oh," Noah said, popping his head back outside. "I thought I'd remind you that I love you," his voice softening. "And I can't wait until we're married."

Ramon turned to face Noah and slowly climbed out of the tub. He ignored his dick, which bounced and ached for Noah.

Ramon curved his hand around Noah's neck and whispered against his lips, "I love you so fucking much," before leaning closer.

6

CHRISTMAS DAY

PIPPA SAT ALONE in the bedroom she had shared with her husband, Elias, for nearly forty-three years. She needed a few minutes to herself; her emotions had gotten the better of her after she washed and put away the dishes from Christmas dinner.

She had five amazing sons, four amazing daughters-in-law, and a son-in-law. At least, that's what she thought the correct title for her youngest son's soon-to-be husband was. But it didn't matter, because she loved them regardless of title. At sixty-three, she had four amazing grandchildren, whom she'd looked forward to for years. This had happened long before her sons found their soul mates.

She chuckled to herself when she thought of Michael with his children. He had three children under the age of three, who kept him and his wife, Lily, on their toes. They'd had a rough month, but the spark was back between them. She was glad she'd kept the young ones overnight to give them time alone. Lily also looked as though she'd found a new lease on life. She needed a break, although Pippa didn't think she'd gotten much of one with Michael while they were away.

And Lucien had never looked happier. Her troubled son finally looked free of his past, which made Pippa's heart feel lighter. She'd worried about him since receiving the call from the hospital about the fire. Pippa had no illusions that Sabrina had pulled Lucien into the light, bringing him his newfound happiness and their baby, Alexander.

One of her favorite Christmas presents was from Lucien, who announced that they were planning to build a home on the family land. It was a permanent home. She actually burst into tears because at that moment, she knew he was living again.

While she was still crying, she received her other favorite gift from Sebastian and Carla—she was going to become a grandmother for the fifth time! They hadn't told her, but instead gave her the present and asked her to open it quickly. Inside, she found two large balls of lemon-colored wool, knitting needles, and a baby-knitting pattern. It took her a while to put two and two together, but when she looked at the glowing couple and noticed that Sebastian's hands were cradling his wife's belly, she finally understood. She really hadn't seen that coming.

It also made her wonder how long it would be before Ruben and Rosie announced that they were expecting. The two hadn't left each other's side all day, much like the other couples.

As she dabbed at her face, she turned toward the door when she heard the handle turn.

Her handsome husband walked in and stopped short when he saw the tears on her face.

ELIAS KNEW Pippa had been upset, and he knew why: she had been overwhelmed by the love in their home.

Pippa had always filled their home with love, and Elias had enjoyed forty-three amazing years with her. He looked forward to the next forty-three. There had only ever been one woman for him. From the moment they met, he never looked at another. Why would he when Pippa held his heart and happiness in the palm of her hand?

He walked over and sat beside her, pulling her into his chest and putting his arm around her shoulder. "I have you, Pip." He kissed the top of her head.

Elias was tall compared to his wife, who was five feet four inches tall, and it seemed to be a trait that his sons had followed because all of their wives were shorter than they were. Noah was around the same height as Ramon, but the girls were small. The best things in life came in small packages, a fact he knew firsthand.

"I'm bursting with happiness. All of our sons look so happy with their partners and children. I couldn't be happier if I tried."

"I know. It feels good to look at them now, knowing we had something to do with making them the men they are today. It's our love that made them who they are. You know that, right?" Elias smiled at Pippa, and his heart beat wildly in his chest.

"I know, honey." Pippa dipped her head back onto her husband's chest. "It's a wonderful feeling, and I'm afraid my emotions got the better of me." It hit me all of a sudden just how perfect our family is. I mean, everyone has their ups and downs—some more than others—but everyone under our roof today was really happy."

"Yes, they were. Speaking of happy, did you notice George? He seems to have a new bounce in his step since marrying Janet."

He felt Pippa chuckle against him. "I did. I'm glad he finally made an honest woman out of her."

Elias laughed. "I think it might have been the other way around, though, to hear Michael tell it. Apparently, she gave him a choice: marriage or separation."

"That would work. The poor man is besotted with her and has been since he worked as Michael's driver."

"He is that."

Pippa moved out of his arms. When her tears had dried, she said, "Do you remember saying, all those years ago, that when we had the money and time, we'd go to Europe?"

He smiled. "I remember it like it was yesterday. You were lying under me in a field of daisies. I'd never seen a more beautiful sight than I did that day."

She sighed with a soft look on her face.

"I think," he began, "it's time we took the vacation

we used to talk about before we got married and had kids."

Pippa smiled and cupped his cheek with her hand. "Thank you for giving me five beautiful sons. I love you, Mr. McKenzie."

"I love you, too, Mrs. McKenzie."

7

RAMON & NOAH

WARNING - M/M SEXUAL EXPLICIT CHAPTER

THEY WERE MARRIED. They were really married. No matter how many times he thought the word "married," Ramon still found it hard to believe that they had finally done it. That they'd made it legal. He had a husband.

Their wedding day seemed to go in slow motion until they said "I do" in front of their friends and family. There had been lots of laughter, as well as tears. His mom had been unable to hold her emotions in check. She let her tears of happiness flow, and of course, that set his sister-in-law's off.

He couldn't fault any part of their day; it went beyond his wildest dreams. He had his mom to thank for the caterer, though. Just the thought of the caterer made him shudder, but not in a good way.

However, being able to celebrate their love with their family at the home where he'd been raised really brought the day together, making it all the more special.

He smiled to himself as he watched the lights of downtown Lexington through the large window of their suite. They had an early morning flight for the first leg of their trip to Mauritius, so they decided to spend their first night as a married couple in luxury.

Noah disappeared into the bathroom as soon as they walked into their room, leaving Ramon to his own devices. He stripped down to his shorts and waited. His dick was so hard he could pound nails. A tingle of arousal slithered along his shaft, dripping from the head and soaking the material of his shorts.

His hips thrust forward, wanting and needing more. Then he heard the shower turn on. That was the signal he needed.

He shoved his shorts down his legs and stalked to the bathroom. The door was ajar, so he pushed it open. He caught his breath at the sight of Noah in the shower. Noah's beautiful body was slick with water, and his cock matched his own in hardness. He felt a desperate need to taste it.

Before he knew it, he had dropped to his knees in the shower and turned Noah around to face him. Within seconds, Ramon had Noah's dick in his mouth and his hand wrapped around the base.

"Fuck, Ramon," Noah groaned. "Don't stop. Fuck. That feels good."

Noah gasped when Ramon took him deeper and swirled his tongue around the sensitive crown. Ramon's cock jerked with arousal, so he wrapped a hand around his rigid dick and stroked it.

"Together," Noah groaned. "Fuck, Ramon. Stop. I want to go together." Noah gasped, forcing his dick from Ramon's mouth.

He held his hand out and pulled Ramon up from the floor. Their mouths met in a passionate kiss as their bodies rubbed together.

Not having had sex for a month before the wedding, they were both crazy with pent-up lust... or passion... or whatever you wanted to call it. Whatever it was, they were about to blow.

Noah slipped his hand between them and wrapped his fingers around their rigid cocks. They both dripped with precum, and as Noah started to fist them, their lust knew no bounds. Ramon gripped Noah's ass, spreading his cheeks, while their mouths stayed glued together. They rutted and moaned. They broke off the kiss, gasping as their cocks jerked and released. Their cum coated their dicks, bellies, and thighs. Then, their tongues met again, and they continued their mating dance.

It took mere minutes, but they finally came up for air and smiled.

"I'll clean you up," Noah offered. He coated his hands with shower gel.

Ramon knew that having Noah's hands on him would make him hard and ready again, but who cared? It was their wedding night. They could sleep on the flight tomorrow.

Just as he predicted, his dick was hard and ready as Noah took his time cleaning Ramon's balls and the area between his legs. When the tip of Noah's finger rimmed Ramon's ass, a sharp curse left Ramon's mouth. He used his hands on the shower wall to keep himself on his feet, with Noah trapped in front of him.

"You're fucking killing me," Ramon moaned into his arm as he pushed his hips forward. He gasped for breath the next instant when he felt Noah's mouth suck the head of his dick. "Fuck me."

"That's the plan." Noah stood up and caressed Ramon from his ass to his shoulders before stepping away. "But I'm ready to get you in bed."

NOAH LAY on top of Ramon, straddling his hips with his legs, their cocks pressed together between their stomachs.

They pressed their foreheads together and looked into each other's eyes, soft smiles on their lips.

It had been an amazing day that wouldn't be forgotten for a long time. Seeing all their family together had been amazing, and even Ramon's cousins from Montana had been present. The biggest surprise was Sylvia, Sebastian's assistant at McKenzie Holdings, wearing an engagement ring from their cousin Eric. It was a pleasant surprise, but a surprise nonetheless.

"What are you thinking about?" Ramon asked, caressing Noah's back.

"Our wedding. Family. Sylvia's engagement."

Ramon chuckled. "Yeah, I knew it was heading

that way, though. I'd seen Eric watching her for a while before he made his move."

"Didn't it bother you?"

"It bothered me that it didn't bother me. If that makes any sense," Ramon admitted.

"It makes perfect sense." Noah dipped his chin and captured Ramon's lips with his.

They had both been craving this closeness, which they had worked hard to avoid over the past month. Now that they were married, though, they had a month to catch up on.

"Tell me how you want this. Anything, Ramon."

Ramon arched as his excitement dripped between them.

"I want it tender. I want you on top of me, my dick in your ass. Most of all, I want it slow." He kept his eyes locked with Noah's while telling him exactly what he wanted.

They'd taken the edge off in the shower, so with a bit of luck, they would be able to make love slowly. At least, Ramon hoped they would.

Noah rained kisses down Ramon's neck, continuing until he could nibble his tight nipples. This caused Ramon to arch into Noah's touch.

Ramon wanted to touch Noah, too, so he flipped

them over and delighted in having Noah under him. Ramon knelt between Noah's thighs, spreading him wide open with his hands. He sucked in a breath at the sight of Noah aroused. His balls pulled tight to his body, and his beautiful cock jutted up toward his navel—hard and silky looking.

Ramon bent down and licked from just beneath Noah's scrotum to the bulging head of his penis. Precum dripped onto Noah's stomach, and Ramon used his tongue to clean it up. He loved how Noah's cock jerked with arousal. Ramon swirled his tongue back down and circled the rim of Noah's ass.

Noah loved being rimmed and found it so arousing that he'd jerked himself off a few times while Ramon rimmed him.

Ramon didn't let up because he wanted his husband to be open and ready to take him. He hollowed out his tongue and breached the tight rim. This caused Noah's hips to twitch and his breathing to become heavy with need.

"Lube," Noah moaned and tossed the bottle to Ramon.

Ramon didn't need any more instruction, so he flipped the lid and poured the liquid directly onto Noah's ass and his own hands. In his haste, the bottle fell from the bed, but he didn't notice. He was too impatient to wait. It turned Ramon on to know what he was doing to the man who was currently enjoying his touch.

Ramon managed to ease a finger into Noah's ass and get another digit in as well. It killed him not to have his mouth on Noah's cock while he fingered him. Noah would blow quickly like that, which was why Ramon stayed away from his groin. He didn't want Noah to come until his cock was inside him.

Ramon groaned, unable to wait any longer. He removed his fingers, crawled up to Noah, and gave the twitching crown a quick swirl of his tongue. They were both hard as granite when Ramon ended up on his back again.

Holding his dick straight, Ramon groaned through the torture of having Noah put on a condom and lube him up before slowly seating himself on Ramon's dick. Ramon panted and tried to lie still. He knew his excitement was at its limit. As soon as Noah signaled that he was ready to move, Ramon did.

He stretched behind him to hold onto the headboard so he wouldn't start jerking Noah off just yet. He wanted to last longer than a minute.

Noah moved up and down a few times with his

eyes closed in concentration, then focused on Ramon. Ramon leaned over and reached for Noah's hands. They held each other's hands tightly and Noah pushed Ramon's hands into the bed on either side of his head.

They maintained eye contact as Noah rocked on Ramon's cock. The friction was insanely delicious, and precum dripped from the end of Noah's dick onto Ramon's stomach with every downward thrust.

"I'm close," Noah hissed between clenched teeth.

"Let me touch you," Ramon begged.

Noah shook his head and whispered against Ramon's lips, "I'll come without," before sealing their mouths together. That was all it took. Ramon came inside his husband at the same time Noah coated them with his release.

AFTER ANOTHER SHOWER, they snuggled up in bed together, but sleep eluded them. They were too hyped up from their wedding festivities to fall asleep. Not even the sex they'd had was enough to knock them out.

"Ramon, can I ask you something we never seem to find time to talk about?"

Ramon lifted his head from Noah's chest and met his gaze. "You can ask me anything. You know that." He frowned and rested his chin on Noah's chest while waiting for an answer.

"Have you ever really thought about adoption?"

Ramon was surprised by the question, especially on their wedding night. He smiled and admitted, "I'd like to look into adoption with you at some point. I know you'd love to have a child, and my family loves kids. Well, my mom especially does, so I'm open to it." Seeing the frown mar Noah's brow, he added, "I love you, Noah. If you want to adopt, I'm with you all the way. But if you don't, I support that decision as well. I'm happy as long as we're together, children or not."

Noah smiled, caressing Ramon's hair before cupping the back of his head. "That's good to know. I was just curious, and truthfully, I'm not sure what I want to do." He pulled Ramon up to meet his lips.

Ramon no longer worried about anything as he rested against Noah's chest. Noah was by his side, and Ramon knew he always would be. His love for Noah was his last thought before sleep finally claimed him.

EPILOGUE

25 YEARS LATER

Pippa sometimes felt her eighty-eight years, but as she watched her family surround her and her husband as they celebrated their sixty-eighth wedding anniversary, she felt tears threaten to fall.

She and Elias weren't as spry as they used to be, but they'd had a good life. Apart from a few health scares over the years, they were both in good health, albeit old.

Pippa's eldest son, Lucien, and his wife, Sabrina, arrived late because they had to detour to the airport to pick up their children, Alexander and Olivia. They had flown in late from Montana, where they had been visiting their cousins. Elias hadn't let on, but he was relieved to see them because he'd developed a fear of flying many years ago on their trip to Europe. Despite Elias's discovered fear of being in the air, that trip held fond memories. She shook that memory free and watched Michael.

Michael spoke to his youngest son, Joshua, who had just turned twenty-three and wanted to apply to the FBI. He dreamed of becoming an agent, which is why he majored in criminal psychology in college. His parents weren't so keen on the idea, but Joshua could talk anyone into doing what he wanted. Pippa knew he'd be an agent one day. Michael Jr. and Charlotte worked at McKenzie Holdings now that their father had retired. Pippa knew Michael would still be around the office; he wouldn't be able to stay away from the company he helped build years ago.

As she glanced at twenty-five-year-old Sirena, a tear slipped from her eye. Sirena was carrying her first great-grandchild, and Pippa was beside herself with excitement. Sirena's husband, Harry, was absent, which bothered her granddaughter. She would find out from Lily what was going on. Lily would know because she always found out about anything involving her children.

"Grandma, are you okay?" Paige asked, passing her a tissue.

"I'm fine. I just get emotional at family parties. Seeing everyone together makes my heart lighter. Which reminds me, where is your twin?"

Paige smiled. "Rachel is over there talking to Dad."

Pippa glanced over and smiled at her handsome son, Ramon, as he talked to his daughter. Paige and Rachel were twins born to Ramon and Noah twenty years ago via surrogate.

Pippa turned back to Paige and asked, "What was going on between you and Dylan?" Her eyes narrowed as her granddaughter squirmed where she stood.

Pippa had seen Paige arguing with Dylan, Sebastian's son and her cousin, not too long ago. The argument had seemed heated until Dylan stormed off, leaving Paige with an angry or resigned look on her face.

"Nothing really," Paige shrugged. "He was trying to tell me what to do, and I didn't like it."

Since Rachel, Paige, Dylan, and Ruben's son Jaxon all went to the same college, Pippa suspected that the argument stemmed from that. She really didn't like arguments between her grandchildren. The McKenzies were damn stubborn when they wanted to be—none more so than her husband.

"Sofia says we have to cut the cake soon, before the topper melts or falls over," Madison whispered, amusement in her eyes.

Madison, Sebastian and Carla's oldest child, had a wild streak a mile long. Pippa knew she was the one who gave her father gray hair. Dylan was usually the calmer one, so he must have had a good reason for picking an argument with Paige.

"Grandma, don't forget the cake."

"I won't, Madison." Pippa took Elias's offered hand and got to her feet. "Tell Sofia to be ready."

"I will." Madison went off toward the kitchen to relay the message.

Sofia was Ruben's middle child, and she looked just like her mother, Rosie. She was set on a career in catering, and her dream was to own a wedding cake business. Sofia was just as strong-willed as her father, so Pippa knew her dream would come true.

She hadn't taken two steps when Ryan, Ruben's eldest son, appeared beside her. "How's my favorite girl?" He kissed her on the cheek.

"Stop trying to sweet-talk your grandmother," Elias mumbled.

She chuckled because they'd been saying that to each other since Ryan was sixteen. She had a feeling that he liked the ladies a little too much, what with his sweet talk and his cowboy swagger. She told Ruben that Ryan was too young to be in Kenza, let alone help run the place, but her son just laughed. Probably because he really was like his father.

"Help me sit." Once she was settled next to Elias, she turned to Ryan. "Why don't you have a girlfriend yet?"

Ryan blushed. "Now, Grandma. I'm only twenty-three; there's plenty of time to find 'the one.'"

"I can see Alexander and Dylan carrying the cake, so you're off the hook for now." Pippa chuckled to herself as a sigh of relief left her grandson.

Reaching her age and still having all her family alive and well touched her beyond anything she could imagine. She knew she was lucky, and not a day went by that she didn't thank God for blessing her with so much love.

Keep reading for the first chapter of Baby Makes Three, McKenzie Cousins, Book One (Sirena McKenzie)

MCKENZIE FAMILY TREE

Elias and Pippa McKenzie
  Lucien & Sabrina
  Alexander 25
  Olivia 23
  Michael & Lily
  Michael Jr 27
  Charlotte 27
  Sirena 25 (spouse Harry 27)
  Joshua 23
  Sebastian & Carla
  Madison 24
  Dylan 20
  Ruben & Rosie
  Ryan 23

Sofia 21
Jaxon 19
Ramon & Noah
Paige 20
Rachel 20

BABY MAKES THREE

MCKENZIE COUSINS #1

SIRENA MCKENZIE (MICHAEL & LILY'S DAUGHTER)

"Michael do you have a minute?" I ask my brother with a wry smile on my face. My brother looks at home sitting behind the huge desk in the McKenzie Holding's building in downtown Lexington. He became CEO along with our sister—his twin—Charlotte, and our cousins, Alexander and Olivia, when our father and uncle Sebastian had semi-retired. I smile at the thought because neither of them have fully retired and not a week goes by without them being in the office breathing down Michael or Alexander's neck.

It irritates Charlotte and Olivia no end because they leave them alone and personally I think it's because they both have a wicked temper.

Michael has always been the more sensitive and he's always the one I go to for help or advice and I know that he will always be in my corner regardless of what I have to deal with. He reminds me of our father in that respect. Michael has broad shoulders and the McKenzie dark hair, and with the dark scruff covering the lower part of his face, the girls go crazy. He's never short of company, but I know he isn't happy. He isn't fooling me.

As I'm trying to read his mind, Michael looks up and smiles. "I always have a minute for my sister," he replies, smoothly. "Come and sit, Sirena. What's up?"

Moving forward, I sigh in relief as I take the weight off my aching legs. "I've had enough, Michael." My chin trembles and I know that my tears are going to be falling soon. "I'm not sure I can do this."

"Oh crap." Michael jumps up and crouching in front of me takes hold of my hands. "I think Mom might be better at this." He winces and truly looks pained.

My brother's panic makes me laugh as the tears finally start. "What am I going to do?" I wail and

Michael looks to the door, probably contemplating his escape or praying for help.

"Oh stop." I tug my hands free. "You're my brother and should be used to us girls by now. You're also a guy and I need someone to explain Harry to me."

Michael sighs and moves to sit beside me. "Harry is an asshole who doesn't deserve to share the air you breathe."

I hiccup and silently cry into my hands. After a few minutes, Michael gently tugs them away and gives me a sad smile.

"Listen to me." Michael starts wiping my tears with his fingers but then gives up and grabs some Kleenex to finish the job. "You are one of the strongest women I know, Sirena. I also think you know what you have to do and if there wasn't a baby involved, then you'd have already done it."

"I just want a man to love me like Dad does Mom. I want him to cherish me and to want to take care of his child and me. I want to be able to return that love tenfold so that he never has to doubt how much I love him. I want that." I dab at my eyes. "And instead I'm married to a womanizing asshole who doesn't remember he's married and that his wife is pregnant with his child."

My brother tightens his jaw in anger on my behalf, but right now I want a solution to my dilemma—do I stay with asshole Harry and try to stick it out until at least after the baby is born, or do I tell him that I'm leaving and will be in touch with him once our baby arrives? Harry probably wouldn't even notice if I just moved out without saying a word.

"I'll support whatever decision you make. Just tell me what you want me to do?" Michael brushes the hair back from my face and smiles. "I have the house by the lake if you want to go there."

"Really?" I let the idea take hold.

At five months along I shouldn't need medical attention for a while and my next OB appointment isn't for a few weeks. "I like that idea." I smile softly.

"Thought you might." Michael's gaze flickers between his desk and me. This tells me he's busy and that I'm holding him up, but in my distressed state, he's being too nice to kick me out.

"I'll go." I hold my hand out so that Michael can lift me from the chair.

He grins widely at the sight of my struggle that I laugh. "Don't you dare say anything!" I glare playfully.

"I wouldn't dare." He chuckles. "Look sis, if you

can get packed up in time, I'll come by after work and help you move."

Reaching up, I tug my brother's face to mine and press a kiss to his whisker-covered cheek. "Thank you."

Michael wraps his arms around my shoulders and pulls me against him. His chin rests on the top of my head. "I love you. You have to promise that if you need anything that you'll call, otherwise I'll take you to Mom and Dad's instead."

"Funny man."

"I mean it, Sirena. You're five months pregnant so it's not just you I'm worried about."

I raise my face to Michael's and place one last kiss to his cheek. "I know and I promise." Moving toward the door, I turn and glance back at Michael. "Can we keep this between the two of us for now." I wave my hand, motioning to him and then back to me.

"Not for long though," he partly agrees with a nod. "Mom will be asking questions soon, and when she doesn't get an answer, I'll have to deal with Dad."

"Give me a few days and I'll call them . . . I'll see you later."

"Take care, sis." He waves me out of his office.

With Michael's promise to help me move out

weighing heavily on my thoughts, the last thing I expect is to find someone else walking down the corridor toward the elevator. Although McKenzie Holding's is a large international architectural and construction company, they like to keep the head office quiet and serene without clients running in to others especially for those clients who require utter most secrecy.

Reaching the elevator, I glance at the man from the corner of my eye and smile when he catches my gaze. His scent, soft and woodsy, floats toward me as he holds his hand out to indicate I'm to enter the elevator first.

He's older than me, perhaps in his forties with light brown hair that holds a hint of grey around the temples. His smile and the amusement in his blue eyes cause me to forget my problems as I sink into his gaze.

"Lobby or parking garage?" he asks with a brow raised.

"Lobby." I sigh, wishing that I'd driven because my body aches.

The doors slide closed and the tall man beside me turns, offering his hand, "Garrett Hudson." He smiles brightly and my heart stutters, my eyes widening in surprise at the flare of unexpected attraction I feel.

I hesitate and reply, "Sirena Bennett," shaking his outstretched hand.

GARRETT

The minute her hand slides into mine my heart quickens, and noticing her stomach is swollen in pregnancy doesn't dim my attraction to her.

She has a head of dark hair that cascades down her back in loose curls. The beautiful skin of her face is lightly tanned and bare of cosmetics. The green eyes that are caressing over my features remind me of the emerald jewel. She's exquisite and so much younger than me that my heart aches. In a way it's also a reminder that I'm being ridiculous.

Sirena still has her hand inside of mine when she clears her throat, a slight blush coats her cheeks, but she makes no move to remove that hand. "You had a meeting with McKenzies?" she enquirers.

I smile and reluctantly release her hand. "I did. Alexander McKenzie."

"My cousin." She smiles.

"You're Michael and Charlotte's sister, right?" I ask, but I already know the answer considering I'd overheard her conversation with her brother.

My heart has ached for years waiting for the same thing that Sirena had sobbed to her brother about. Someone to love me and to give me the family I crave. My bank balance has always gotten in the way of my want.

"That's me." Sirena smiles, but it slips and then disappears altogether when the elevator comes to a screeching stop. "Oh God! This isn't good."

"Don't panic," I glance at her and then to the panel at the side of the door, "please. I've got this." I try to reassure her as I place my briefcase on the floor and grab the emergency phone. "They'll have us out of here real soon," I try to calm her, hoping that I'm right.

The minute someone answers I quickly explain our situation. "They're working on it." I look at Sirena and notice that she's rubbing her back and trying to hold her panic inside. "Do you need to sit?"

She looks at me, her anxiety clear in her beautiful eyes.

"I think I better." She glances at the floor and

looks around so I follow her gaze and wonder what she's looking for because the floor of the elevator isn't all that bad. I guess we should be thankful for small mercies.

"Sirena, are you doing okay?" I ask and feel my heart constrict when I notice the tears on her face. "Tell me how to help you."

She bites her lip and looks so forlorn and embarrassed that I'm tempted to take her into my arms and hold her close. My fists clench to keep them at my side as I await her response.

"I'm not sure how I'm going to get down there." She caresses her belly, and I understand the problem at once.

"Let me help you." I smile to put her at ease and wait for her to acknowledge my offer.

Sirena nods and a small smile appears on her face.

Stepping closer, I slip one arm behind her back and take hold of her arm with my other. "Go slow," I advise.

In slow motion she leans into me and we gradually have her sitting comfortably on the floor. After removing my jacket and tie, I join her and instead of sitting opposite like I should have done, I sit beside her and smile.

"Talk to me, please," Sirena begs. "I'm not usually claustrophobic but I feel as though I'm going to start panicking soon if I'm not distracted."

"I'm not much of a talker, but for a beautiful lady, I will make the exception." I smile, which deepens when I notice the blush she tries to hide by dipping her head.

"Okay then, well—"

She chuckles at my poor attempt to start the conversation. "I'll go first." She lets me off the hook. "I've been married for thirteen months to a man who doesn't want our baby or me. I've known from the day we were married that I was making a big mistake but I went ahead with it anyway." She sounds so sad, but I stay silent because I want to hear it all.

"I'm now five months pregnant and later today I will be leaving our apartment and him for good. The sad thing is that I'm not even sure he'll notice that I'm not there." She shrugs. "My parents have the perfect marriage and that's all I've ever wanted. I want to love and be loved by that one special man, but so far my judgment sucks." She goes silent and then turns to meet my gaze. "I'm scared, Garrett."

"Why?" As I ask her that question I realize that I want to take away her fear, no matter the cost.

"I'm scared of this pregnancy even though I'm excited to have a baby. I'm scared of being alone and not having any support from the baby's father, though I'm not sure I even want it. I'm afraid that another man won't want me because I will come with the baggage of another man's child. I'm scared of a lot of things that I never thought I would be."

Her confession hits something inside of me and I want nothing more than to help her, to make her see that she's beautiful and will find everything that she craves one day. Ridiculous as it seems I wish with all my heart that I were years younger and able to offer her everything. My life has always been centered on work, and real love has always been missing.

Reaching for her hand, I enclose it within both of mine, wanting to offer her comfort. "Your husband is an idiot to throw away a life with you." I offer her a small smile.

"Thank you for saying that."

"I mean every word, Sirena." I flex my fingers around her hand and turn away before I say more than what we'll both probably be comfortable with. "My turn."

She chuckles and moves her hand to intertwine our fingers together. Her touch is so soft that my body floods with arousal, which I close my eyes to try and hide.

Clearing my throat, I admit, "I'm forty-nine, Sirena." I glance at her and notice a frown cross her smooth brow. As I continue, I wonder whether my age bothers her as much as her young age bothers me, "I've never been married, although I've come close and had a lucky escape. I haven't been in a relationship for too many years to count because I'm sick and tired of someone wanting to be with me because of my name as opposed to me as a person. It gets tiring, and although I'm lonely it's for the best."

"You said that they want to be with you for your name, why?"

My head rests against the elevator wall and when I turn to look at Sirena she meets my eyes. "I own a small chain of luxury hotels and villas," I admit. "All everyone sees are dollars signs." I chuckle bitterly.

"Instead of the man beneath," Sirena adds. "That's a shame."

Silence follows and as I let it wash over me I realize that I've admitted more to Sirena in those few sentences than I have to anyone else. I also have a feeling that she has done the same when she talked about her bastard of a husband.

"What do you think is taking so long?" Sirena asks and starts to fidget.

"I don't know. Are you okay?" My body turns toward her and I catch a wince of pain flicker in her eyes.

"For the past month I get back ache and it can get rather painful." She lets go of my hand and slips it against her back.

I can't bear to see her in pain so I quickly stand and hold my hands out to her. She glances back and forth between my hands and my face and then slips her hands into mine.

With a tug I have her on her feet and turn her to face the wall. "Take your jacket off and I'll rub your back for you. I can't just watch you suffer."

She hesitates but then her jacket comes off and drops to the floor.

"You really don't have to do this." She bites her lip, which I see through the mirrored wall.

"I know I don't," I whisper as my gaze wanders over her slender back and curvy bottom that leads to legs that I'll be dreaming about later.

I push back my arousal and slowly start to rub her lower back. I clamp my jaw shut tightly in determination to be nothing but respectful toward her. Her hands rest against the wall facing us and when she moans in pleasure it goes straight to my balls. It doesn't help when I watch her reaction through the mirror and notice the tight buds of her nipples against her thin shirt. My eyes quickly lift to her face and that's when I feel a blush start to rise up my neck at having been caught.

"Sirena," I whisper.

"I know." She dips her head so when I slowly start to massage up along her spine, I move her hair to the side and place a kiss to the nape of her neck.

She shivers and presses against my hands as I continue to massage her lower back. I move my lower body away so that she doesn't discover exactly what her moans are doing to me.

"Oh, she kicked." She smiles and presses a hand to her stomach.

I watch in amazement as her baby kicks and stretches in the safe confines of her mother's belly.

Our eyes meet and she nervously chews on her swollen lip, which drives me crazy. I want it to be my mouth that chews and licks along her deliciously plump lips. It makes me sad to realize that it will never happen—can never happen.

"Do you . . . um, want to feel her kick?" she offers

and my fingers twitch. "It's okay." She smiles. "I think we've gone past the awkward stranger stage."

Sirena taking my silence as agreement, slips her hand over mine on her hip, and slowly slides it up to her belly and holds it close. My body heats at being so close to her and blood rushes south at the feel of her against my front . . . and then her baby pushes against my hand and her smile lights her face and does something to my heart.

"A miracle, Sirena," I whisper into her ear as my other hand goes to her hip to keep her close. I nuzzle closer and inhale the subtle scent of her apple shampoo.

My eyes go to the mirror and the look of arousal on Sirena's face as her eyes drift closed causes my hands to tremble, the want running through my body.

I know this is wrong but I want this one moment in time with this beautiful woman. I kiss the curve of her neck and move my hand from her hip to cover hers on the wall. Our fingers intertwine and the fingers of my other hand spread over her belly.

Sirena opens her eyes and locks on to mine, letting her head drop back against my shoulder. She turns her face up to meet mine . . . and the elevator makes a sudden and loud cranking noise before it starts to move downwards.

I curse softy under my breath and slowly step away from her, making sure that she doesn't stumble. "Let me help you." I grab her jacket from the floor and help her back into it before scooping up my own and grabbing my briefcase.

Knowing that I can't leave her without someway of getting in touch, I ask, "Cell phone," and hold my hand out for it.

Sirena looks almost relieved when she passes it over and watches me input the numbers. "My home number is in there along with my personal cell number. If you need anything . . . anything at all call me. Even if you only want someone to talk to." I pass it back to her and the doors swish open.

"Sirena." In a whirlwind of movement, her brother dashes inside and wraps her up in his arms. "Are you alright? The baby?"

Holding my gaze over her brother's shoulder she smiles. "Thank you," she mouths and pulls out of her brother's arms.

I don't hang around to listen to them because my need to be the one taking care of her is driving me crazy, and I know that I will never be able to do that. I also know that my sudden feelings toward her are ridiculous.

Making my way down the stairs to the parking garage, I quickly climb into my car and then curse a blue streak because I forgot to get her number. At the time I was more concerned about her being able to contact me.

I hit the steering wheel and curse again when my cell buzzes in my pocket. I want to ignore it but unfortunately with the completion of my new hotel nearing I can't.

The damn thing won't stop buzzing with messages now my cell reception has reconnected, but I find a grin splitting my face when I see an unknown number, with the words: *Thank you. Sirena x*

I now have her number, which I quickly save to my contacts. I do pause though when I slip my cell back into my pocket as my brain engages. All I see now is the twenty plus years between us, which is a lot more than a small problem.

With a mirthless laugh, I rest back against the seat of the car knowing that I'm being stupid. Sirena is a beautiful young woman and surely wouldn't have even looked at me if we hadn't of gotten stuck in the elevator together.

Who are you trying to convince?

She was interested.

I'm not going to dwell on it because the chances are that I won't see her again, and I'll just put this afternoon down to a brief encounter. It doesn't change the fact that for the first time in a very long time, I felt happy.

BABY MAKES THREE is available at online book stores.

LOVE IN MONTANA

DE LA FUENTE #1 (MCKENZIE SPINOFF)

SYLVIA

THE MUSIC BLASTED through the nightclub as the crush of bodies on the dance floor went wild. They thrashed around in a sensual frenzy, which drew the attention of Sylvia and her friend, Russian-born, Talya.

As the music pulsed and slowed, the lights dimmed to almost dark. If it weren't for the colored spotlights, Sylvia wouldn't have been able to see her friend, who stood beside her.

Sylvia sighed as she rubbed her temple. She was tired and, after the long workweek, had wanted to curl up in her pajamas and read. Instead, Talya had persuaded her to go out with her and that was why she was dressed in a short, skin-tight, dress that barely covered any of her assets.

Once dressed, Talya had dragged her to the club. She'd love a drink, but the last thing she really wanted was to cloud her judgment with alcohol. She didn't want a pick-up, or a one-night-stand; she just wanted to dance.

Sylvia knew the owner of Kenza, Ruben McKenzie, because she worked for the McKenzie brothers, mainly, Sebastian and Michael. And there was the youngest brother, who had taken her out around town for a while, but she sensed something was going on with him. At one time, she'd imagined things would get serious with Ramon, but they hadn't. And because of that, she'd started to let their cousin, Eric De La Fuente, get under her skin.

She didn't know why. Eric hardly had anything pleasant to say to her, he usually just glared. On the odd occasion that he opened his mouth, snide remarks would pop out. That he disliked her so much when she couldn't get him out of her head was annoying.

"You're doing it again," Talya shouted into her ear.

She frowned and wondered what her friend meant. What was she doing again?

"Thinking too much." Talya grinned, and grabbed hold of her hand, pulling her onto the dance floor. "Think while dancing."

Sylvia could do that.

The bodies already taking up space on the tightly packed dance floor, writhed together, and the ones closest to Sylvia appeared lost in a sexual haze. Not wanting to be caught staring, she closed her eyes and let the beat pull her under.

Her arms rose into the air as she started to move like only a professionally trained dancer could. Her body shimmered with an air of mystery and the sensual pull kept her where she was, song after song. The music flowed together and she wasn't aware of the crush of the crowd or when the song changed, all she was aware of was the beat and the way it pulsed through her veins. She lost herself in the music, lost her sense of time. Strong hands gripped her hips, snapping her back into focus. She froze. Her eyes snapped open and were captured in the angry green ones of Eric.

Although Eric was related to the owner, Kenza was not a place she'd ever expected him to be. He seemed more like a quiet bar with a beer in his hand kind of guy.

Unable to hold his gaze, Sylvia tried to step out of his grasp, but he dragged her into his body, and insinuated a leg between hers. Her dress crept up but stayed covering her ass when his large hands clamped down on her bottom.

She quickly grabbed hold of his shoulders for balance, and to keep herself upright because being so close to him had turned her legs to Jell-O.

The music had her blood flowing, but being so close to an aroused Eric caused the blood in her veins to overheat—and aroused he was. There was no mistaking the length of his cock, which throbbed against her hip as they rubbed together in sensual heat.

She'd never danced with anyone the way she was with Eric. His hands kept her riding his thigh, as his fingers brushed the hem of the dress and made her skin crave his touch. Her fingers twitched to reach down and grasp his hard dick. Instead, she slid her fingers through the hair at the nape of his neck and brought her chest flush with his.

Her nipples were hard, aching tips, which he'd feel as she rubbed against him. She'd never been so aroused while dancing before, and Eric had her ready to orgasm.

With each movement, their groins rubbed together, and it wouldn't surprise her if Eric could feel how wet she was through his jeans as her pussy rode him. It had been so long since she'd had sex, and something told her that sex with Eric would be like nothing she'd experienced before.

Wait! What the hell was she thinking—contemplating?

Moving her chest away from his, she tried to put much needed space between them, but then his gaze captured hers. She wasn't going anywhere. It was a look she'd never seen reflected toward her before, and she wasn't sure that she had the strength to walk away from him.

He brought her back against his chest, and growled into her ear, "I've tried keeping my hands off you." He sucked her lobe into his mouth.

She gasped in pleasure as her arousal flooded her thong.

"I've been watching you since I spotted you lost in your own world. I couldn't help wondering what it'd feel like to have you dance on my cock."

He shouldn't talk to her like that. Like he wanted nothing more than to find a dark corner to fuck her.

It was clear that he was ready for that. *Ugh—the image!* She squirmed in lust and tried to close her legs, forgetting that his was between hers, and then she caught the knowing smirk on his handsome face.

"Let me take care of you." He rubbed his chest against the twin peaks of her breasts, drawing a hiss from her lips in protest.

She couldn't pretend that she didn't want him since the evidence spoke for itself. She wasn't so far gone that she didn't realize tonight with Eric would be a one-time deal.

The sensuous feel of having a virile male body— hot and hard against her—played with her common sense because she wanted to say yes. She wanted to go some place with Eric and let him fuck her senseless. Something told her that he fucked like he went about his daily business—*full speed.*

Her back hit a wall. When Eric's hands slid up her thighs as he wrapped her legs around his waist, she stopped thinking and went with the flow.

His large cock felt so good against her wet pussy that she didn't even mind having her dress around her waist.

Reaching up, she pulled his head down to hers, and as their mouths joined, a whole lot of fireworks exploded behind her closed eyes. They snapped open in shock, and stared into his passion hazed ones.

She could feel the warmth of his jeans on her folds as the thin fabric of her thong had been pushed to the side from her grinding. All she wanted was for him to open his jeans and impale her; finish what he started.

It wouldn't take much to send her into complete bliss. She just didn't know how to ask for what she wanted. What she shouldn't want, but couldn't get out of her head.

Groaning, she searched out his tongue with hers and sucked—hard—pulling it into her mouth. He hoisted her further up the wall, and his fingers... searched, and found...and then she came back to her senses.

She wasn't into a public sex show, which is how her dance with Eric had turned out. At least she came back to her senses before it was too late, and he was inside her.

She briefly closed her eyes at the thought of him being buried between her thighs. Because the idea of his huge cock, as it slid back and forth inside her, caused her vaginal walls to clench with hunger.

Slowly, Eric realized that she was no longer taking part, and, as he struggled to catch his breath, his eyes met hers. Before his mask of anger slipped back into place, hurt flickered in the green depths.

"You'll never belong to Ramon," he growled as he lowered her to the floor.

"I know that." She didn't want him thinking she'd stopped because of Ramon. "We're in a club." She laughed. "We're not even in private. I didn't stop for any other reason but me remembering where we are."

"Bullshit," he shouted in response. "You stopped because you don't want word getting back to Ramon that you got down and dirty with me."

"That's—"

"The truth. I know your history with him, and I'm telling you that nothing will ever come of you being with Ramon."

"Don't presume to know what I'm thinking. I wanted you. You big idiot." She shoved him in the chest with her finger. "If you'd started that outside my apartment then I'd have dragged you inside to finish what you started, so don't go making excuses up for me. I don't need one."

Well, that argument had slightly cooled her libido. He really was an idiot. In fact, she was one as well for letting him bewitch her on the dance floor. Her head was always full of him, so she would never say no to having his hands on her.

She felt more screwed up than ever. She knew Ramon was out of the picture, at least where a relationship was concerned. But before tonight, she had no idea that Eric wanted her. In fact, she thought he hated her.

She shook her head to clear it of the emotions that tried to drown her. How the hell would she be able to forget the feel of Eric against her? Or how it felt to have his hands on her ass?

"Sylvia, Eric," Ruben greeted, having suddenly appeared.

Thank God it wasn't a few minutes ago.

"Ruben. How's Rosie?" She asked to distract him from the knowing look he passed back and forth between Eric and her.

Ruben grinned, wide. "She's amazing. It's her night off tonight or I'm sure she'd have enjoyed the show." He smirked, but looked at Eric as he cleared his throat.

Oh, he saw.

Her face heated, but she decided to turn it into an opportunity to prove to Eric that she hadn't stopped because she didn't want Ramon to know.

"I'm going, and Ruben, feel free to tell your brothers about what you've just seen. This ape," she glared at Eric, "is under the impression Ramon is the reason why I stopped, but it isn't."

She pushed past Eric, and hissed, "Ass," over her shoulder.

He glared in her direction, and she felt his eyes on her all the way to the exit where she met up with Talya.

"He's not finished with you," Talya observed as they left.

INDECENT VILLAIN
A DARK MAFIA ROMANCE

My parents descended into the ground while I stood
motionless and unresponsive to the penetrating
darkness that was Tiberius Beckett.

He moved into my home and I realized that the man
had two sides, and he showed me his true face. I liked
him. He became my obsession, as I became his.
Together, we did some bad things.

Do you want to know more about Tiberius Beckett?
Then let me tell you about my indecent villain.

Available Now!

PROLOGUE

KINSLEY

Fragile.

I feel like I'm going to fracture into a thousand pieces.

I stand silent and motionless beside my parents' graves, rain soaking me to the skin. The wind whistles around my body as I remain unresponsive to the penetrating darkness directed at me by Tiberius Beckett, my father's brother. The man stands tall in his dark suit, his piercing gaze seeming to search for something within me, as if he knows a secret I'm not even aware of. Despite the storm raging around us, his presence feels more unsettling than the howling wind.

My tears mix with the rain and flow down my cold cheeks. The priest speaks loudly and clearly, but his words blend as my mind refuses to comprehend them. I swallow hard as my mother's casket is lowered into the earth. Then that of my father follows. It is the end for them, and for me, too. Tiberius, at my father's request, has become my legal guardian. He doesn't want me, just as I do not want him. I tell myself I'll endure for the next two weeks until I turn eighteen. It's not long, but it feels like an eternity.

I pray that I survive the man with silver eyes.

But no one survives Tiberius Beckett.

TIBERIUS

Fragile.

Kinsley looks like the wind will blow her over any second. The girl does not trust me. She will. My fingers yearn to stretch across the space between us and take her in my arms. I am a hard man. But with Kinsley, my heart is fucking mush. She is my vulnerability. The girl has been in my head for a while now. It kills me to stand here and watch her suffer alone.

She is unaware of the danger she is in, just as she is unaware that my men are hidden around the cemetery to keep her safe. Me too. However, they know she is their priority. I can take care of myself, but

Kinsley cannot. She needs me, even if she doesn't realize it yet.

The rain falls harder as my brother and his wife are now in the ground. Other mourners and the priest take their leave, while Kinsley and I remain. I stare at her. Kinsley lifts her face, her eyes finding mine. I don't look away, and neither does she. We stand there in silence as the rain soaks us both. In that moment, I know that I will do whatever it takes to keep the defiant young woman safe, even if it means revealing my true feelings.

CHAPTER ONE

Three days after the funeral, the rain continues to fall. The gardens have turned into fields of mud, and even the long driveway has puddles. My grand home looks gothic surrounded by the dark clouds and rain, but in the sun, it is beautiful. I've always found the house to be too spacious for our small family. The house once bustled with numerous servants, but that was before my time and before my father's as well. Grandfather used to tell me about the garden parties his mother hosted when he was six. Sadly, not long after that, there was a war. He said most of the servants left and took up arms for their country—mostly the men, but some of the women did too, I guess.

Sighing, I consider my predicament. Tiberius is a strange man and has the power to unnerve me. I think back to my younger years but can't really put my finger on when I started to feel that way. Maybe it had more to do with my father being unsettled around his brother than anything else. I must have picked up on his unease and let it affect me. However, Tiberius does nothing to help dispel those feelings around him. I think he enjoys it. I'm not like my father, though. I won't let the man push me around. I may have been showing weakness since my parents died, but no more. I'm not a little moth who needs nurturing. I'm nearly eighteen years old but feel older.

If I'm honest with myself, there is a slither of happiness within me that I will no longer be held prisoner in my home. My parents were afraid of something in the months leading to their deaths and had kept me home with a private tutor. I don't miss the city, but I do miss going into town, even if it is only for a cup of coffee while I watch the world go by. It's better than being locked up inside the Lake House.

I press a hand to my stomach, trying to quell the bundle of nerves that suddenly rises as I watch a large black car appear through the trees along the drive- way. The wheels kick up muddy water as Tiberius brings the beast to a stop close to the front entrance. Another car, this one silver and sleek, pulls in beside the black one. The man has arrived, along with my parents' attorney.

Tiberius climbs from the driver's side of the car, while another man emerges from the passenger seat. They exchange words.

The attorney, Mr. Arnold Fielding, exits his car and runs for the front door. Tiberius takes one step and seems to be frozen to the spot. His head suddenly turns, and his gray eyes lift and find mine. Stunned, I gasp, but I refuse to look away first. My heart thumps heavily behind my breastbone. How did he know I was watching, and from where? He snaps his atten- tion back to his passenger, a man in jeans and a tee. Unnerved, I head into the bathroom and splash cold water onto my face. I pat it dry with a fluffy towel. The mirror before me reflects my drawn expression. Dark circles are prominent beneath my eyes, the color matching my long hair.

A knock on my bedroom door draws my attention. I swallow hard, knowing there will be no escaping the next hour or so. Today is the reading of the will, followed by lunch with Tiberius. I am overjoyed.

Another knock.

"One moment," I shout.

I slide my feet into the shoes I kicked off earlier and take one last glance in the mirror. The dark color of my midi dress does nothing for my washed-out look. I open the door and catch the impatient look on the housekeeper's face.

"About time," Martha snaps before briskly turning away.

I roll my eyes and inhale, holding my breath for a few seconds before slowly exhaling. It helps center me when I know I am about to face danger. That is what Tiberius Beckett is to me—the devil himself.

And there he is.

His dark-gray eyes follow me as I move down the staircase, his body remaining still like a predator. I refuse to let him see the nerves that threaten to break me in his presence. He is the kind of man who, if you give him an inch, he will take a mile.

I come to a stop at the end of the stairs and hesitate. My father's office will be used for the reading of the will, and the thought of being locked behind closed doors with Tiberius and the attorney makes me want to run. Of course, I do nothing of the sort. I am an Elliot. I can do anything.

At that moment, Mr. Fielding appears.

"My dear, Kinsley," he says as he moves, taking my cold hands into his much larger and warmer ones. "I am sorry for your loss. Come and take a seat." He leads me into the office and sits me in a Queen Anne chair in front of the large window. The choice of seating arrangement surprises me, as the meeting table would have sufficed. Nevertheless, I accept the small cup of coffee he places in my hands.

"Thank you for your condolences. It is a very difficult time," I acknowledge, trying to act the way my mother would want me to—like a lady instead of a rebel. I lean forward and place the cup on the coffee table.

"Mr. Beckett," Mr. Fielding calls, "please take a seat beside your ward."

I cringe. I do not want to be his ward, nor do I want him sitting beside me. From his hesitation, I gather he doesn't want to sit beside me either. He takes the seat opposite, which is even worse. He won't miss anything now.

Mr. Fielding clears his throat and shoots an impatient glance toward the evil man. "Let's get started, then." He unbuttons his blazer and sits, a sheaf of papers in his hand. "Kinsley, you are aware that you are now the ward of Tiberius Beckett, at your father's request."

"For two weeks. Yes, I am aware."

My gaze lifts to the man in question. His hard face shows nothing of what he is thinking. Those dark eyes of his rove over me in a way that causes my heart to pound. The sneer on his cruel lips sets me on edge. As we are, it is the first time I have been close to the man. He looks younger than I first thought. Early thirties to what I previously labeled as early forties. His thick black hair curls over his ears. High cheekbones are marked by a scar across one of them. His rugged features give him a dangerous air, but there is a fleeting hint of vulnerability in his eyes. Have I misread them? The way they narrow on me, I think not. He hates that I've seen it. Despite his intimidating presence, I feel a flicker of curiosity about the man who now holds power over me.

A throat clears, which forces my gaze away from Tiberius. Mr. Fielding clears his throat once more. "The last will and testament is rather brief, I am afraid." He looks at me over the rim of his glasses perched on the end of his thin nose. "Your father wasn't one for time-wasting."

"Get on with it," Tiberius growls as his tattooed hands clench his thighs.

"It is a joint will with your mother." Mr. Fielding clears his throat again, which is becoming annoying. "We hereby leave all our assets to our daughter, Kinsley Elliott. The house we also leave to our daughter—"

"What?" Tiberius questions in a quiet but deep voice as his attention snaps to the attorney. His eyes narrow. "He left the house to"—he turns and glares my way with hatred—"her?"

The papers shake in Mr. Fielding's trembling hands. "That is what he wrote."

"What is going on?" I ask, annoyed. Why would Tiberius be upset that my parents left our family home to me? It makes no sense. But then it makes no sense that I would be left as Tiberius's ward when the man had made my father nervous.

"You want to know the truth, little girl?" he sneers and stands. He shoves the coffee table out of the way and leans over me, his hands tightly gripping the arms of my chair. When he is so close that I can see silver mixed in with his dark-gray eyes, he says, "The house was supposed to be left to me. I had an agreement with your father." His eyes blaze with emotion. "I have your father's signature on the agreement between us."

I'm trying to concentrate as Tiberius is making a point, but all I can think about is the heady scent of his cologne. It seeps into my senses and gives me ideas I should not be having.

"You smell nice," I blurt.

His brows shoot up to his hairline as he tightens his jaw and takes his seat, his face on the lawyer. "The house is rightfully mine. I won't sit back and accept this," he scoffs. "Even in death, he's doing his upmost to fuck with me."

I place a trembling hand on my stomach while I fight to get my equilibrium back. His reaction confuses me. I don't want to draw attention to myself, but I must ask, "Why would you think you're entitled to this house?"

"Because," he grinds out, "the house belongs to the oldest living male relative. With Jude gone, that is now me. It's the way it has always been done."

"Why didn't I know about that?" I ask softly, feeling like my family betrayed me. "I don't understand my father. I have only ever seen you from a distance, but now I am your ward. Why?"

Tiberius frowns when his eyes land on me. "None of that matters now."

I force my gaze to the lawyer. "If Tiberius thought he was getting the house, then am I correct to assume my father made a previous will? What was in it?"

"That doesn't—"

"Tell her," Tiberius snaps.

Mr. Fielding takes a sip of the glass of water in front of him, and says, "In your father's previous will, he left the house to Tiberius Beckett and explained why. As Tiberius said, the eldest male descendant was to inherit the house."

"My father was Jude Elliott. How are you a Beckett?"

"That piece of paper in your hand will not stand up in court when I have my lawyer file an objection." The man totally ignores me and speaks to Mr. Fielding.

A headache brews behind my temples, and I want to leave the room. I feel sorry for Mr. Fielding, who has done nothing but read my parents' wishes. Tiberius reminds me of a bull ready to charge. His nostrils flare, and his large body tightens with suppressed anger. He is a tall man who obviously takes good care of himself. The muscle he possesses is unable to hide behind the clothes he wears.

I sense the tension in the room escalating as Tiberius's anger becomes palpable. I need to diffuse the situation before it escalates further. My hands feel sweaty and my mouth is dry, but I have to say something to calm Tiberius down.

"I don't want the house. He can have it." I rush the words out and bring the two men to silence. In truth, the house is the only home I've ever known, but I always planned to leave when I turned eighteen.

"What?" Tiberius shakes his head. "What did you say?"

I swallow hard, and say, "You can have the house." I turn my gaze to Mr. Fielding. "You can arrange that, right?"

"Actually"—the older man sighs—"nothing can be done until you turn twenty-one."

Tiberius releases a string of curse words, some of which raise my eyebrows in shock. As difficult as it is to ignore his strong presence, I turn away from him and give my full attention to Mr. Fielding. I need to concentrate.

"I'm assuming there is a clause about selling the house."

"It states that you must live in the house until you turn twenty-one, after which time, you can leave and pass on ownership. However, your father stipulated that ownership could only be passed to Tiberius Beckett."

"Let me get this straight. My father left me the house, yes?" He nods. "But I have to continue living here until I turn twenty-one, at which point he expects me to hand the house over to him." I point toward the beast of a man.

"That is correct."

"Why didn't he just leave the house to him in the first place? This doesn't make any sense." I get my unsteady legs under me and stand. "What about college? How will I go if I must live here?"

"That detail we will discuss at another time," Tiberius says, calm once more. He takes out a piece of gum and moves it between his fingers. Is he trying to quit smoking?

"My father was afraid of you." It takes courage, but I manage to hold his gaze. "Why would he make me your ward?"

"I'm the only one who would have you."

"That's not quite—"

"Mr. Fielding," snaps Tiberius. "Thank you for your time this morning. I will bring my niece into your office next week to sign the documents you have for her." He ushers the lawyer from the room.

My refusal to join Tiberius for lunch has garnered his anger once more. The man takes my arm and drags me into the formal dining room, where he pushes me into a chair beside the one at the head of the table, which he takes.

"You need to eat." His large hands tighten around his cutlery. "You've lost weight since the last time I saw you."

In truth, I am hungry. The food in front of me looks more appetizing than anything Martha has prepared since my parents died.

"Hmm," I mutter as I straighten in the chair and start to eat. Tiberius watches me with a calculated look on his face as he continues eating.

The food is pleasant, which puts me at ease and leads me to ask, "Will you be moving in?"

He nods.

"Good. At least we'll get something edible."

He pauses with a fork of beef near his lips. "Explain that comment." He places his knife and fork on the plate and sits back, his gaze unwavering.

"Since my parents died, the food hasn't been good." I sigh. "I'm not allowed in the kitchen to make my own, so it's no wonder that I've lost weight. I hate tuna, which Martha serves me on crackers for lunch daily."

"I shudder at the thought," he says. In his next breath, he shouts, "Martha!"

The woman who hates me comes dashing into the room. "Sir?"

My cheeks flush hotly, and I silently plead that he won't drop me in it with her. Tiberius narrows his eyes on my face, and his jaw twitches.

"I will be moving into the house later today, and I expect breakfast and dinner served in this room with my niece daily, unless otherwise stated. There will be no tuna and crackers." He pauses for a moment, holding her full attention. "There will also be no seafood put on the table. Ever."

Martha shoots me a look of hatred before she says, "Yes, sir."

"My niece is the owner of this house, which means

she is your employer. If you value your position here, I suggest you treat her with respect. She needs to eat, not starve. Do I make myself clear?"

"Yes."

"Yes, what?"

"Yes, sir."

Tiberius snorts. "Go." He turns to me. "I have no clue what I am supposed to do with you."

"You could ignore me, and I will ignore you."

He grins, which surprises me. He has to be the most handsome man I've ever seen. "You're too pretty to be ignored, and I'm too big and loud." He frowns. "Others will be moving into the house with me. You need to stay out of their way." He points his fork in my direction. "They are dangerous men. I will only give you this warning once. You understand me?"

It's a good thing I've eaten all my food, as my appetite suddenly disappears. "I understand." My mind whirls, wondering who they are and why he has dangerous men living with him. My outlook is certainly looking better. Maybe I won't be bored anymore. Tiberius is a large man with an equally large personality.

As my eyes rove over his features, I realize I don't consider him my uncle. How could I when I've never known him? My curiosity about him is piqued, and while he seems slightly more approachable than he has been in the past, I decide to ask my questions.

"Are you married?"

His gray eyes shoot to mine. "No." He smirks. "Are you?"

"Considering I'm seventeen, I would have thought the answer to that question was obvious."

"If you ask me personal questions, then expect the same in return." He grins, mirth dancing in his gaze. "What else do you want to know?"

"Why have we never actually met until now?" I sit back in the chair and try to appear relaxed. I certainly feel better than I did before. Maybe I just needed something proper to eat, or what I do not want to admit, company. I'm not sure how I feel about Tiberius. That's a lie. The man with silver eyes causes parts of my body to come alive. Butterflies flutter in my belly. Maybe it's the way he looks at me. I have his sole attention, and I want to keep it.

"There are things that your mother chose to keep from you. I need some time to decide whether or not I tell you what they are."

I watch him, my curiosity stronger than ever. "Would those things change anything?"

He sits forward with his hands on the table. He intertwines his fingers. "The secret Anna and Jude kept would change everything," he says in a deep voice, his eyes blazing. "One day, I may tell you."

I frown. If I'm not mistaken, I catch something within his gaze, as though he is scared to speak of it. I'm more determined than ever to discover what my parents kept from me.

"Not today?"

"Maybe not ever." He stands and tosses his napkin on his plate. "If I do tell you, just remember they are the ones who kept you in the dark." With that, he moves toward the large doorway. He pauses with his hand on the knob and glances over his shoulder. "I will be here from this evening."

"You!" Martha hisses the moment the large front door closes behind Tiberius.

To my horror, my legs tremble at the confrontation I know is seconds away. Martha has always been an evil woman. As soon as Tiberius spoke to her, I knew she would be on me the moment he left. And here she is.

"How dare you complain, you ungrateful little bitch!" Martha charges forward, and I stumble into the wall behind me. She follows and slaps me hard across the face.

Tears fill my eyes as I cradle my throbbing cheek, too stunned to react.

"You think it matters to me that you own this house?" she scoffs. "You know nothing." Her eyes glow with unleashed anger. "I would be careful of who I become friends with, Kinsley," she sneers. "Beckett is—"

I watch her closely as her mouth pulls tight. My heart pounds in my chest while I wonder how to break free of her hold. Martha has never laid a hand on me before, but now the woman before me is finally showing her true colors. I pull myself up to my full five-foot-five height and glare at the woman.

"Do not touch me again," I say, clear and precise. "Next time, I will fight back."

Her eyes narrow. "You are brave all of a sudden." She scowls and looks out of the window. "I may not like you, but if the rumors about Tiberius are true, then I fear for you." Her arm shoots out and holds me against the wall. She is stronger than she appears. "No more whispering into that man's ear about me, or you will be very sorry." With one last shove, she turns and leaves.

I gasp and give into the tears that have been threatening to fall throughout the whole confrontation. My cheek stings as I place it against the cold window and watch the dark clouds roll over the grounds. My stomach is in turmoil. I don't understand what is going on. The one fact that I do know is that I am the ward of Tiberius Beckett. Why him? I have no idea why my father did that. Although I do not trust Martha, her words have me concerned. What does she know about the man to fear for me?

Something else has become apparent. My father knew he was going to die. The changes to his will were completed three weeks before his death. The weight of my new responsibilities as Tiberius's ward settles heavily on my shoulders as I consider the implications of my father's foresight. The realization scares me.

Scared and out of my depth, I turn away from the window. The grandeur of the dining room now seems suffocating, a stark reminder of the impending gloom that arises within me. The portrait of my father hanging on the wall seems to mock me with his knowing gaze, as if he has left behind secrets that I am now forced to uncover. The feeling of unease grows stronger, making me question everything I thought I knew about my family.

Somehow, I manage to pull myself together. I will not let Martha see how much her sharp words and slap across my face have affected me. The woman will not be working at the house for much longer if I have my way. Maybe Tiberius has his own staff that he can bring here. Anyone would be better than the bitter Martha Green.

CHAPTER TWO

I tear off my suit and change into jeans and a tee. After fastening my biker boots, I release a frustrated growl. I don't know what the fuck to do about sweet, innocent Kinsley.

I glare out of my bedroom window, my gaze settling on the house across the lake. I open the door and step out onto the balcony. It's sparsely furnished, with just a table and two chairs, plus a comfortable chaise lounge chair. I've spent many summer nights asleep on it. The outdoors has always called to me, just like the Lake House has.

Memories always swamped me whenever I

dropped in on Jude and his family. In recent years, my brother had become uneasy about those visits, which made me wonder what he might have been hiding.

As I rest on the balustrade and gaze out once more across the lake at the house, I wonder what Kinsley is up to. It's something I've wondered for a while now whenever my eyes caught on the house. Thoughts I should never have, even now. At first, it was innocent curiosity about the girl I knew my brother hadn't fathered. But over the past couple of years, I found myself unable to stay away. I've never been introduced to the girl until now. I made sure I always stopped by when I knew she wouldn't be home.

Kinsley grew up rather quickly and became a stunner. I shouldn't be obsessed with her. It's wrong. I know that what I'm feeling would be considered acceptable in the real world, if it weren't for the age difference. I'm not really her uncle. Never have been. Never will be. She doesn't know that yet.

One look at me covered in tattoos would disgust her. My brother never liked ink. Neither had my mother, which is why I have so many.

Kinsley doesn't remember, but when she was told about her parents' deaths, I showed up at the house. She was in shock, so I took charge of her. I held her while she stared into space. I held her some more when her tears finally came. I held her while she slept.

I should have stayed with her so she wasn't alone, but I was dealing with my own grief. Not only that, but I also had to deal with the cops and make arrangements for Jude and Anna. I took my grief and anger and went after the crew who had forced my brother's car off the road. His brakes had been cut, and as the crew chased after them, Jude wasn't able to slow down on the sharp bends of Snake Pass.

I saw the bodies and wish I hadn't. The only bit of luck that evening was that the car hadn't burst into flames.

One crew member was still at large. That was my fault. I lost it with the three my men and I had found. The last one died before he could give me a name. However, I did get one name from the other two. Cannon Edge.

That bastard would pay one day.

I turn my head at the sound of booted feet moving down the hallway outside my bedroom.

"Boss," Salem shouts, knocking on the door. "You in here?"

"Outside," I yell.

He strides out and comes to rest beside me, his gaze following mine. "Do you know what you're doing?"

"I don't have a fucking clue."

He snorts. "I haven't seen you this fucked up before."

I glare at my friend. "I'm not fucked up." My eyes stray back to the Lake House. "Edge is going to come for Kinsley."

"He won't get her. Between you, me, and Jock, we've handpicked all the men who will be around the house. She will be safe."

"Tell the men they don't touch her. Make sure they know she's my family and I will personally kill anyone who causes her harm."

"Yes, boss," Salem drawls, mirth in his voice, which I ignore.

"Prick!"

"Edgar has the weasel in the basement. You wanted to talk to him."

"I want to do more than fucking talk," I snarl.

"Who is he?" I ask Edgar.

The man tied to the chair, with blood and sweat running down his face, is not familiar to me.

"Brinkley," Edgar growls. "I overheard him bragging about knowing where Jubal is hiding out. Why the fuck he'd do that is anyone's guess."

I narrow my gaze and clench my fists. "He's either stupid for flapping his jaws or doesn't know shit, which also makes him stupid."

The man spits blood on the floor. "Fuck you! I know who you are, and you and that bitch will be next."

Before the asshole can blink, I slam my fist into his face. The chair wobbles and then crashes backward.

"Where the fuck is he?"

Although the man laughs, fear sets in. I see it in his eyes and the piss stain on his jeans.

"I lied." He laughs. "I fucking lied. I don't even know who Jubal is."

I crouch beside him as I wipe my hands on a cloth. "You see, I don't believe you. With both mine and Edge's men looking for Jubal, it would be fucking idiotic to lie about knowing him." I glare at the piece of shit and force myself to stand. To Edgar, I say, "Find out what you can. Then turn him over to Edge."

"No way." Brinkley tugs against his bindings, struggling to break free. "He'll kill me."

Edgar laughs. "Beckett didn't say you have to be alive when I turn you over to Edge."

Pure fear erupts on Brinkley's face.

I walk away. Salem, who had kept to the background, says, "Something doesn't add up with that asshole."

That is what I've been thinking since Edgar brought him in.

Five minutes later, my phone beeps with a message from Edgar. I read it twice before sharing the info with Salem. "Edgar sent the location Brinkley gave him to Prez to get the murdering asshole."

"Fucking hell! Brinkley really was an idiot."

I trust Prez to find Jubal now. All I must do is wait. Something I've been doing since Jude died.

"Make sure the bikes are loaded on to the truck. I don't want to be traveling back and forth between the houses for now."

"They've already been loaded. When do you want to leave?"

"Now."

Salem heads off to round the men up while I stand outside in the fresh air. In truth, I don't want Kinsley in this world of mine, but whether I do or not, it doesn't matter anymore.

Kinsley's life is now tied to mine whether she likes it or not.

CHAPTAER THREE

I watch as four large black SUVs come up the driveway. My heart thuds in my chest with a mixture of fear and excitement. Tiberius said he would be back.

The moment he steps onto the gravel driveway, his head lifts, and those dark-gray eyes of his land on me. I don't move, and neither does he, until another man says something to him. I shake myself, questioning how the man can ensnare me so easily.

Men in jeans and tees climb from the vehicles. Out of the nine men I count, two are wearing dark suits. Tiberius has changed out of his suit into black jeans and a white tee with sunglasses perched atop his head. It's certainly a different view of the man than the one I previously had. Who are the men with him? They all look dangerous and unapproachable. Surely, they're not all moving into the house.

My head turns as I hear booted feet enter the house. Tiberius gives instructions in a loud voice, and then the footsteps start upstairs. My bedroom door is locked, but that won't keep anyone out who is determined to get inside.

A moment later, there is a knock on my door. "Ms. Kinsley, your, um, uncle, would like you to come downstairs."

I frown at the door. The voice is hesitant, which is not what I expected. Suddenly, more curious than scared, I dash to the door and pull it open. My eyes shoot wide at the huge man standing before me in a lovely dark-gray suit. He is most certainly not what I expected after the voice I heard through the door.

He smirks. "Call me Jock," he says in a calm voice. "You must be Kinsley." He holds out his hand and smiles, but then his eyes narrow as he zeroes in on the side of my face that is red and bruised. "Who did that to you?" His voice deepens.

"The girl is accident prone," Martha says, appearing out of the blue.

The large man stares into my eyes, and I silently beg him not to say anything because I know that he knows who is responsible. He turns to the woman. "Martha, isn't it? You are wanted in the kitchen." When she hovers, he adds, "Now, woman!"

I wince, which Jock notices. "She won't touch you

again. Come. He's waiting for you." I nod, trying to hide my nerves as I follow Jock down the dimly lit hallway. "Don't worry too much about the men in the house. They will leave you alone."

I hesitate at the top of the stairs. "Maybe I should have changed first."

"Nonsense. You look fine." Jock smiles. My eyes travel down my white tee to where my black jeans cling to my skin. Thick socks cover my feet. I didn't bother with my biker boots today.

"Stop fidgeting," Jock says as he shoves me into my father's office—what was my father's office. The heavy door closes behind me. If I didn't know that Tiberius was already in the room, his scent would have given him away.

"You look scared," he comments.

I turn around. "It's unnerving having strange men wandering around my home."

His eyes narrow, and then he is suddenly in front of me. A large, tattooed hand holds my jaw as he turns my face to get a better look at the bruise forming there. I doubt Martha intended on leaving such a sign that she'd hit me.

Tiberius looks into my eyes. "This is because I

called her out at lunch." His jaw tightens. "I'll get rid of her."

"No!" I grab hold of his wrist before I snatch my hand back. A sizzle of electricity shoots up my arm. I swallow hard. "I mean." I sigh. "I don't know what I mean."

His fingers gently smooth over the soreness of my cheek before he steps back. "That woman—"

"Boss," a dark-skinned man interrupts us. He grins when he sees me, and I don't think I've ever seen anyone with such perfect, white teeth before.

My lips twist into a smile when I realize the man is really being friendly. "Hello," I offer.

Tiberius narrows his eyes between the two of us and snaps, "Saul! I do not pay you to drool over my"— he clears his throat—"niece."

"No, sir!" Saul snaps his focus to Tiberius, who hasn't stopped glaring. "I came to tell you the truck is five minutes out."

"Okay. Get them moving once they arrive."

Saul nods and exits the room without another glance my way.

"Are the men moving in as well?" I ask the silently brooding man. I try to ignore the fact we're dressed similarly. Thank God I left my boots off; otherwise, we'd be identical.

"Yes." He enters my space, and it takes all my will power not to back down. "You will not encourage them."

It takes me a moment to understand what he is saying. When I do, my eyes widen in surprise. "He's far too old for me." I don't add that my taste in men centers on the man in front of me.

"So dramatic." He steps back and looks irritated. "Regardless, do not speak to my men."

The sound of a loud vehicle approaching breaks the silence as the wheels crunch on the driveway.

I look out the window and frown at the eighteen-wheeler. "What is in there?"

"Furniture, among other things." He pauses in the doorway. "Do you want any of the furniture from your parents' bedroom before I have it destroyed?"

"No, thank you." That is something I do not want. "However, if you wish to get rid of my father's desk, I would like that."

He nods. "Dinner will be in an hour or so."

❄

"Why don't you step away from the window?" Jock suggests.

"I'm curious. I've seen Tiberius every now and again over the years; however, I never actually met him until the reading of the will. I mean, he was at the funeral, but we didn't speak. My father thought he was doing the right thing by making me his ward. So, I must trust in that." It doesn't stop me from admiring the fit of his jeans and tee as he moves.

"Your father knew Beckett would protect you if he asked. You will be safe here."

I turn to Jock and frown. "You call him by his family name?"

"Habit." Jock smiles. "How about a warm drink in the kitchen. I could do with a cup of coffee myself."

"Okay." I follow beside him and come to a stop. "What are they carrying upstairs?"

"A bed."

"He doesn't want to sleep in my parents' bed, so he brought his own." I glance at Jock for confirmation.

He nods.

"I suppose that makes sense." I sigh. "There are a lot of things that do not make sense to me, though. Many in fact, and I don't know where to start."

"Let's have that cup of coffee," he suggests and

leads me toward the kitchen. "Problem?" he asks when I come to a sudden stop before stepping foot inside.

"I've never been allowed inside the kitchen," I whisper.

"From what I have been told, this is your house, which means this is your kitchen." He smirks and pushes his way inside. A growl comes out of his mouth when he sees Martha at the far end of the room. "You lay a hand on this girl again, and I will show you how hard a man as big as me can hit."

Oh God.

"You took the words right out of my mouth, Jock." Tiberius moves into the room. "This is your last chance, Ms. Green." His steely eyes narrow on the woman before he shoots a look I can't decipher at Jock. "Do not bring my niece over to the dark side while I'm in the office."

"Wouldn't dream of it."

Tiberius snorts and turns his attention to me. His eyes linger as he grabs an apple on his way out of the room.

Jock claps his hands. "Show's over. Now, can someone show us where we can make our coffee?"

"It's behind you. Nothing too fancy," a timid voice replies.

I turn to find a former employee. The young woman is maybe three years older than me. She's also the daughter of one of Martha's friends, and I'm sure she fears the vile woman too. "Thank you, Marie." I smile at her. "I didn't know you were working here again."

"Mr. Beckett called the old staff back." Marie moves closer. "I am sorry about your parents, Kinsley." She grabs my hand and squeezes.

"Thank you," I say, choking on the words.

I turn my attention to Jock, who's pouring two cups of coffee. He passes me a cup, then places a hand to my back and guides me back out along the hallway.

"The girl seemed nice," he says when we reach the living room.

"Marie is." I sit at one end of the sofa and inhale the rich aroma before I take a sip. "This is very good."

"I made it, so of course it is." He chuckles. "No one comes between me and my coffee."

"Did Tiberius ask you to be nice to me?"

His eyes dance. "He told me not to let you out of my sight."

"Hmm," I mutter.

I sit back and listen to the men putting the bed together upstairs. Hammering comes from the office, which I ignore. I don't want to know what other changes are taking place. Instead, I wonder about Jock. I sense the man was truly angry when he discovered I was hit. He will follow Tiberius's orders in the end, which means I can't trust him as much as I want to. It would be nice to not be so alone anymore.

I guess I will be safe from the outside world in the house. But will I be safe from Tiberius?

Available Now!

ONE OF SIX

A DARK ROMANCE

Six brothers

Six heartbreakers

Six Den Hollows

Essex Redd, the youngest of six brothers at the age of nineteen. My father was murdered four years ago, and we know who did it. What we don't know is why. Things get complicated when I fall in love with the killer's daughter. As the truth begins to unravel, I realize that Bea and my family are in more danger than anyone thought.

My name is Beatrice Alexandria Lincoln. I prefer to be called Bea. I live in the town of Mount Sterling, which is known for its old-fashioned charm and Southern hospitality, and residents like my parents keep those traditions alive.

I long for a life of my own choosing. When my mother dies suddenly, my eyes are opened to the harsh reality of what it truly means to be a Lincoln.

My father has no idea what I will do to protect the people I love.

Available Now!

CHAPTER ONE - BEATRICE

Beatrice Alexandria Lincoln. This has been my name since the day I was born eighteen years ago. My parents, Richard, and Elisabeth are patrons of the town of Mount Sterling in the Deep South. Sweet tea, served with a side of sweet fancy, is the official offering to visitors to the house.

I often wonder if anyone else would appreciate my life more than I do. My father is the one who bought and paid for my entire existence.

We live in a white mansion, a five-minute walk from the edge of town. It's where the wealth is. Lush gardens, sleek and shiny vehicles, designer flower beds, and fake people. The town of Mount Sterling is known for its old-fashioned charm and Southern hospitality, and residents like my parents keep those traditions alive. Despite the material wealth that surrounds us, I sometimes long for a simpler life. My father is the mayor. My grandfather is the judge, and my uncle is the sheriff. You see what I mean?

The residents want to be in my parents' circle of friends. They push their offspring in my direction, hoping that being my friend will bring them recognition. I don't bother anymore. I have one friend and she's enough. It can be lonely living in a community where people are more interested in your family position than who you really are as a person.

I feel like a robot. A Stepford wife. Every waking moment is planned, even more so since I graduated from high school. I want to go to college. Not that I am interested in any field, but to get away from my family. I'm not sure that is going to turn out to my advantage, as my parents are against it. If my parents hadn't been on my back all the time about grades, maybe I would have fought harder. But now it's too late.

My skin itches against the cotton fabric of the dress I wear. The humidity makes sweat run between my breasts and down my back. The weather makes me sleepy as I listen to the drone of my mother and her three closest friends. The suffocating feeling of being trapped in this picture-perfect life is overwhelming. I long for freedom, for a chance to discover who I really am beyond my family's expectations.

Today's meeting is for them to decide which of their sons I will date first. I don't want to date any of them. I have no choice. Richard Lincoln has spoken. I feel like a pawn in their game of social status and tradition, with no say in my own future. The weight of their expectations crushes me.

I smile in all the right places, only half listening. A loud vibration shakes the China on the dining room table. My eyes wander out the window as a slight smile appears on my lips. Motorcycles roar past the house. The men who ride them live across the railroad tracks in Den Hollows. There are no white mansions with manicured lawns in Den Hollows.

I want to be free like them. Free to ride like the wind through the town without a care in the world.

Seconds later, my dream shatters as the sirens announce the arrival of the sheriff's deputies. I sigh, wishing my uncle's deputies would leave the men alone.

They are real men. No tailored three-piece suits covering their pasty white—sometimes overweight—bodies. Jeans and T-shirts cover their muscular frames. I imagine it's one of them every time I use my vibrator.

A blush covers my cheeks as I turn my attention

back to my mother. I wish I'd paid more attention, because ten minutes later they agree on something I missed.

As mother walks them out, I go to my bedroom and close the door with a huge sigh of relief. I throw the clothes off and into the hamper. In the shower, I scrub my hair to get the hairspray out, which Mom insists on before I scrub my body until I'm red and clean.

When I'm done, I brush out my red hair and put on shorts and a vest. I go downstairs barefoot and follow the sound of my mother's voice into the kitchen.

She gives me a scathing look, her mouth tight. "Beatrice, I asked you to be polite. I didn't expect it to be so difficult for you."

"I was there. I served the sweet tea and the fancies. I smiled and spoke when spoken to. What did I do wrong?" I clench my fists behind my back, angry at the words I force from my lips when I want to say so much more.

"Honestly, child." She grabs my arm and drags me through the house. "My friends noticed when you were distracted by the window." Her eyes narrow. "Those Redd boys and their gang of thieves."

"They're not thieves, Mom." The second the words are out of my mouth; I feel a sharp pinch on my arm. "Ouch."

"You watch what you say to me!" she snaps. "Your father was right. You need a man to keep you in line."

"I'm eighteen. I want to go to college and get an education." I pull my arm free, feeling the bruise already marking my skin. "Dad said he would think about it."

Mom sits down. "Yes, well, your father has thought about it. You are going to get married. We can keep an eye on you here until that happens. Make sure you stay pure for your husband."

My mouth falls open.

"Oh, Beatrice, stop catching flies." Her eyes sweep over me in disgust. "You have a date with Jason Greenwood tomorrow night. You will behave like a lady or face your father. Do I make myself clear?"

"Jason? Isn't he old?"

"He's a respectable lawyer in town. He just turned thirty." Her eyes narrow. "Didn't I ask you a question?"

"Yes, Ma'am," I say. "I'm clear." Inside, where no one can hear me, I scream.

"Instead of sulking around the house, go to the store and buy some milk."

It's on the tip of my tongue to tell her to go get it herself in her nice, air-conditioned car. But I don't. My dad's hand hurts bad.

I take the ten dollars she hands me. "Get yourself something to drink so you don't faint on the way home."

As soon as I slip my feet into a pair of ballet flats, I step outside, and the heat envelops me. This summer is hot.

The houses I pass make me sick. None of the people who live in them deserve it. They don't care about anyone but making more money for themselves and kissing my family's ass.

I walk through the gates that are supposed to keep others out, wondering which guard will lose his job because the men from Den Hollows rode through. The men ask for trouble by doing what they did today. Part of me doesn't blame them. If I was told to stay away from somewhere, I'd want to go. The only difference is that I wouldn't have the courage to do it.

I walk through the pretty town, past the barber shop, the post office, and the library on the corner. I cross the street and pass a few restaurants and the sheriff's office. I turn right and walk towards the big grocery store.

The store is quiet as I enter, and I take a moment to stand under one of the air conditioning units in the ceiling. My eyes go wide when I catch my reflection in a mirror. My red hair is completely dried and sticks up everywhere. There is no rhyme or reason to it.

"Beatrice, how are you?"

"I'm fine, Mr. Gleeson. Mama sent me for milk." I sound like my ten-year-old self. "And a popsicle." I like the owner of this store. He has always looked the same—slim, with a head full of white hair, a big nose, and dark eyes that miss nothing hidden behind large black specks.

He smiles warmly, revealing a row of perfectly straight teeth. "You always liked the popsicles."

"I deserve two today. Or maybe three."

"You know where everything is." He smiles. "I'll ring you up when you're ready."

"Thank you." I move away but pause. "Mr. Gleeson?"

"Yes, Beatrice."

"Did you see Den Hollows come through town?"

Mr. Gleeson's smile falters slightly before he answers. "I'd have to be dead not to know when they ride those bikes." He winks. "The sheriff's men chased them right back out of town."

"Oh!" Disappointment settles in my stomach, and I'm not sure why. It's not like I know how to talk to them. If I did, I would feel my father's hand afterwards.

I walk over to the popsicles, pick out a pink one and bite into it with my teeth. As soon as the popsicle bursts it's wrapping, I lick it slowly, savoring the taste. I close my eyes and sigh with pleasure. I wrap my tongue around the ice before taking it into my mouth. It tastes so good.

The sound of a growl makes my eyes open wide. My heart stutters in my chest. The Redd brothers stand on the other side of the store with all eyes focused on my mouth. It has been a long time since I have seen one of them. I don't think I've ever seen them all together—Atilio, Nico, Boone, Galen, Ridge, and Essex. Six brothers. Six heartbreakers. Six Den Hollows.

CHAPTER TWO - ESSEX

My eyes focus on the girl with the brightest hair I've

ever seen. I know who she is. Everyone does. Beatrice Lincoln. The mayor's daughter.

My instant response to her has nothing to do with her parentage, but the girl herself. Curves to make a guy's mouth water. Curly hair that falls in a mess around her face and down her back, over her breasts. It's more orange than red. Fiery.

What freezes me and my brothers to the floor is the way her tongue curls around the popsicle in her hand. The way she licks with her pink tongue, and then heat slides through me when her mouth wraps around the ice.

My dick is so hard that I need to pound something. Preferably into her sweet pussy.

She lifts her gaze and sees the six of us standing watching her. When her eyes land on me my dick jerks behind my zipper. I have never had such a visceral reaction to anyone before and it makes me angry.

Just my luck it's the one girl none of us can touch. Probably one of the only virgins to graduate high school.

I glance at my brothers and wonder what they're thinking. How can one innocent girl bring the six of us to a stop.

Ridiculous.

Still, no one moves.

"Gleeson," I shout. My brother to the right jumps, but I bring us back to the present and the reason we are here.

The girl grabs up two more popsicles, turns, grabs some milk and then high tails it toward the exit.

I feel like I can finally breathe.

CHAPTER THREE - BEATRICE

Mr. Gleeson runs toward me as I head for the exit. I toss him the ten dollars and head for the door. I stop. What if Mr. Gleeson needs help?

I'm not sure how long I stand in the doorway, but the next thing I know I'm being grabbed from behind. I don't even struggle when I look down and see strong hands leading to leather-clad arms around my stomach. When I inhale, the man behind me even smells wonderful. I'm tempted to turn my face to his neck and take another whiff. He'd probably think I was crazy if I buried my nose there.

"Aren't you going to fight me, little girl?" His rough voice breaks me out in goose bumps.

"Atilio," Mr. Gleeson's voice makes him turn around so we're both facing the shopkeeper. "Please put Beatrice down. She's a good girl. Not like..." he winces.

The tall man is the oldest brother, only twenty-six. He was born Atilio Junior, but when his father died four years ago, he dropped the Junior. At least that's what I heard. I may not see the Redd men, but I know all about them. I'm good at listening when others think I'm not.

"I like it in his arms." He starts to move and Mr. Gleeson winces as we pass him. "Make sure the doors are locked."

He carries me to the back of the store where his brothers are waiting. They are all handsome men with a mixture of dark and medium brown hair.

"She's checking us out," another brother says with a grin on his face and amusement dancing in his bright green eyes.

I narrow mine. "I wonder who I should kick in the balls first," I reply.

His eyes go wide, and he moves in front of me. "I can assure you that if you ever get near my balls, you will either be on your knees sucking my dick or on your back with your legs spread."

"Dipshit!" one brother slaps the younger one on the back of the head.

"Excuse Ridge, all his manners were knocked out of him years ago when Atilio dropped him on his head."

"Fuck you, Boone!"

"Guys," Mr. Gleeson appears. "Leave them alone. Atilio, put her down. Ridge, your mother needs to wash your mouth out with soap and water."

My feet hit the ground so suddenly that I lose my footing. Another brother steps forward. "I'm the nice brother. Ignore my twin. I'm Galen." He holds out his hand.

I take it quickly as he begins to pull away. "I'm Beatrice."

His face splits into a huge grin. "Your popsicles are melting."

I blink, surprised.

"Stop flirting," Atilio says. "We've got shit to do." He grabs my hips and sits me down on a freezer lid. "You, don't move."

"Okay." I look into his brown eyes and see flecks of gold. *He has kind eyes,* I think as he pulls away.

I'm curious about what's going on here. Mr. Gleeson isn't afraid of them. So, they can't be robbing the store. Atilio and his brothers are bigger than me. They are over six feet tall. They all wear jeans and a T-shirt with leather jackets of different styles.

I know who each of the brothers are, even though this is the first time I've met them, or rather, the first time I've been in the same room with them.

I absentmindedly tear into another popsicle, sucking out all the melted liquid before pushing the last piece of ice up. I tilt my head and wrap my tongue around it before sucking it into my mouth. It's a little too long to fit, but I crunch it down.

"Those damn things should be illegal in your hands," Atilio says, rearranging his crotch. My eyes fly to his as my face flushes with heat. He gently removes the last one from my hands and smiles. "My brothers won't get shit done if they're busy watching these getting sucked into that pretty mouth."

My cheeks burn. "What are you doing here?" I ask, watching them start to read the labels on the crates in the back of the store. Anything to get their attention away from me and my mouth.

"Looking for something," Boone tells me, his dark eyes fixed on my legs in the shorts I wear. I'm surprised my mom let me out of the house in this outfit. It's tight and shows my curves in a way my mom wouldn't like.

Do the Redds like the way I look? I'm sure they're as curious about me, as I am about them.

"Found it!" a voice shouts.

"Don't drop it." Nico.

The sudden banging on the windows of the store freezes their movements. Mr. Gleeson gasps. "It's the sheriff." He goes pale.

Only one thing to do. I shuffle forward. "I suppose you have a truck in the back?"

"What of it?" Essex, the youngest, hisses and takes a step toward me.

Atilio holds out a hand. "Cut it out."

"If Mr. Gleeson doesn't open the front doors, the sheriff will drive around the back."

"She's right." Boone.

"Let me go out there with Mr. Gleeson and open up. I'll think of something to distract him. Just please don't leave until his car is gone." I wince. "My father will be furious if he finds out I helped you."

"We can't trust her!" Essex argues.

"I trusted you not to hurt me. I have no quarrel with you. Let me do this." I look at Atilio.

"Don't burn us," Atilio says.

"I won't." I look at each brother in turn, remembering which face goes with which name.

Mr. Gleeson takes my hand and pulls me through the store. "Are you sure, Beatrice?"

"You've always been kind to me, Mr. Gleeson, without asking for anything in return." I stop to wave to my uncle. "I'm doing this for you and them. They don't deserve the town treating them the way they do."

"Thank you." He slides the key into the lock. "If you ever need anything, come to me, okay?" He meets my gaze briefly.

I nod as my uncle bursts into the store. "Sheriff," Mr. Gleeson stutters. He sounds angry, and yes, my uncle notices.

"Uncle David," I rush forward and hug him. Something I haven't done in a long time. I guess Mr. Gleeson isn't the only one acting strange. "I'm so glad to see you. I don't suppose you have a few minutes to give me a ride home. It's so hot out, and my mother wants some fresh, cold milk."

Shut up, Beatrice!

"Why was the door locked?"

"Oh, I was helping Mr. Gleeson lift some boxes in the back, and he's alone in here today. We're done now." I smile. "A ride home, please?"

He's quiet and looks between us. "Get the milk."

"Thanks!" I say happily and run to get another carton of milk. I can't even remember what happened to the one I was holding when Atilio grabbed me.

As I get another, I look behind me and see Essex watching me. I'm not sure what to make of him.

"Beatrice!" Uncle David calls. "I haven't got all day?" His voice comes closer as Essex fades from view.

"Got it." I turn down the aisle and find Uncle David coming toward me with a panicked Mr. Gleeson trailing behind. "It was nice to see you again, Mr. Gleeson, I'll make sure to stop by more often."

Uncle David grunts and puts a strong hand on my shoulder. "You don't need to shop here anymore, Beatrice." He leads me out of the store and shoves me into the back of his patrol car. My heart races as the door slams shut. I tell myself I can survive this short ride.

I'm helping the Redds get out of town. I'm doing something rebellious. A first. My father will not be happy when he finds out. He won't be happy if anyone tells him what I wore into town either.

Uncle David gets behind the wheel and gives me a long look through the rearview mirror. His eyes make me want to squirm, but I don't. I can't go anywhere anyway.

Instead of heading home, he stops in front of the sheriff's office. I frown. "Why did we stop?"

"I work here. Enjoy the scenery. I'll be back...eventually." He climbs out and enters the office without looking back.

What! The! Hell!

I reach forward and slam the gate between the front and back of the car. I lean back in the seat and kick the door. I can't believe this is happening. My heart is racing as I realize I may be in more trouble than I thought. I must get out of here. Not only am I scared, but it's so hot. The air is stifling. In a panic, my hands slide along the inside of the door, trying to find a way out. I shout in frustration, then scream in terror as a hooded figure appears at the window. I put a hand over my mouth to muffle the scream.

The door opens. "Essex?" I mutter.

He glares. "Go! Now!"

I scuttle out of the car, dragging the stupid milk with me. I don't hang around to find out where Essex went. I crouch down and sneak past the sheriff's office, then dash along the street.

There will be so much trouble when Uncle David finds me gone. I hope no one saw Essex free me.

Sweat soaks my clothes as I run through my yard. My face is flushed, and I feel overheated. Entering the house through the kitchen door, I drop to my knees and roll onto my back. Panting, I give Evelyn—our maid—a thumbs up so she knows I'm okay. I'm in doubt, mind you, because my heart is pounding in my chest.

"What on earth happened, Beatrice? Have you been running in this heat?"

Tears fall. "Uncle David locked me in the back of his police car. I couldn't get out. He left me there." I cry, not caring if Evelyn sees me.

"Oh, dear." She walks away and I hear the faucet turn on and a few seconds later turn off. She crouches down beside me and presses a cold, wet towel over my eyes and forehead. "Calm down and you'll cool off faster."

"I feel like such a baby."

"You are not. What your uncle did was cruel. He knows that confinement in small spaces scares you."

"He parked in front of the sheriff's office." I sit up and move so I'm leaning against a cabinet. "He left me there. It was so hot, and the air conditioning was off. I couldn't get out, Evelyn."

"He obviously came back and set you free."

I shake my head slowly, my eyes holding Evelyn's. "He doesn't know I'm gone yet. At least I don't think he does."

She frowns. "Then—"

I lean forward and put a hand over her mouth. I whisper, "Essex Redd showed up and opened the door."

Her eyes go wide. "Are you sure it was him? I can't tell the younger boys apart."

"I'm sure it was." Wasn't it? He didn't look like someone who would help me. He'd rather stand there and watch me suffer.

"You mustn't mention his name to your parents. I'm not only thinking of him, but also of you."

"Don't worry, I won't mention the Redds at all."

"Good, now why don't you clean up while I pour you an iced tea."

"I'd like that, Evelyn."

As I get to my feet, the older woman pulls me into her arms. "At least you haven't seen the other boys in town. Your daddy would go crazy."

I flinch, which she catches. "I can't tell you. I promised."

"Beatrice, I fear for you if anyone finds out."

"It's okay." I put my arms around her. "I won't see them again, so don't worry.

CHAPTER FOUR - ATILIO

As soon as my three youngest brothers enter the kitchen, my eyes narrow. They come to a stop. "Which genius opened the door of the cop car and let Beatrice out?" Evelyn had told me the girl thought it was Essex, but he would never do that. My eyes go to Galen.

So, I am surprised when Nico comes out from behind the door and declares, "That genius was me." He grins. "The girl freaked out in the car. It was hot as hell." He shrugs and comes fully into the room. "I grabbed the sweatshirt Essex was wearing earlier and pulled up the hood. Nobody saw me but the girl." He grins. "And she thinks it was Essex."

"You idiot," Essex hisses. "Why the hell did you let her think it was me?"

"It wasn't intentional."

"No one sees or speaks to the girl again," I say. "She's off limits."

"Are you claiming her?" Ridge asks.

"She's the mayor's daughter, and her family runs Mount Sterling. So, no, I am not claiming her. She is young and naive. Stay the hell away from her."

"I was planning to," Essex admits.

"Regardless of this little conversation, I liked Beatrice. It can't be easy for her to have him as a father," Galen says. "She didn't blink an eye when we surrounded her. She helped us get away. She's cool."

Ridge puts an arm around his twin's neck. "My twin likes her." He grins.

"Enough! I don't tell you this often, but I will now. Stay away from her."

These idiots love to mess with me. The thing is, I've learned that if I'm not specific and cover all the bases, they're sneaky, and that doesn't change with age. That's what happens with five brothers.

Mom comes in from the back of the house and as I watch her, I wonder how she survived the six of us.

"What now?" she says.

I subtly shake my head at the idiots. "They set their sights on an unattainable girl, that's all. I told them to stay away."

"Hmm."

"You didn't have to tell me." Essex glares. "Her father killed ours."

Mom gasps knowing who he refers to, a hand to her chest. I jump up and go to her, but Essex is there first. "I'm sorry, but it's true."

"No." She pats Essex's cheeks. "Do not blame Beatrice for her father's misdeeds. Evelyn Park works in the Lincoln Mansion. She adores Beatrice. I won't hear a bad word about her." Mama still has that 'look' that shuts my brother up like nothing else can. "Now leave Atilio alone and clean up the mess you tried to hide in the garage."

Once we're alone, Mom adds, "You should find yourself a nice girl. Someone to take care of you. You took on a lot when your father died. It worries me."

"I found a nice girl today," I add, remembering how Beatrice Lincoln felt when I held her close.

Mom gives me a somber look. "Take your own advice and stay away from the girl. If you go after Beatrice, you will only bring yourself grief. Her family will bring a lot of trouble that none of us can handle."

"I understand that. I was teasing." I get up from the table and kiss Mom on the cheek. She stands and pulls me into her arms. "You're a good son, Atilio."

Mom rarely gets emotional, but when she does, it hits me. I kiss her cheek before pulling away. "I'm going to help them clean up." I pause in the doorway and turn to face her. "Beatrice, why is she so unhappy?"

I surprise her, and worry lines appear on her face. "Atilio," she whispers.

"Please, Mom, tell me."

"She will be married and pregnant within a year, all arranged. The sweet, innocent child is not free to live the life she wants... Please do not look in her direction."

I hold mom's eyes for a while. I want to reassure her that I'll never see Beatrice again, but that's impossible when the girl piques my interest. She showed no fear when I took her in my arms. And the way she ate those popsicles should be illegal. I doubt I'll be the only one having wet dreams about her tonight.

"Don't worry, Mom," I say before heading outside. As I do so, one of my brothers leans against the wall near the kitchen window. I frown, "You heard everything?"

He starts walking toward the garage. "Yeah, I heard. I hope you are planning on listening to Mom." He stomps off.

I grimace and watch Essex go.

Available Now!

LOVE STRYKER

MMA ROMANCE

When my childhood friend, Cora, dared me to write a sexy novel about a martial arts fighter, I agreed, albeit under the influence of alcohol. It was something for me—something different and exciting.

It was supposed to be research, pure and simple. But then I met him—a six-foot-six mountain of a man with no name. The way his muscles flexed and rippled when he trained made my belly quiver. The way his dark hair flopped over his forehead made me want to brush it back from his strong face. His nose had been broken, but it made no difference, he was still a handsome man. He had eyes dark as the night that would land on me the minute I entered his gym…Every…Time.

He was their star fighter, the one that brought in the big money. At first I feared him because of his size and the way he would look at me. But then I discovered that I was his biggest distraction, and no matter what my head told me, my heart told me to fight for the man who didn't know how to live outside of the cage.

NYT & USA Today bestselling author Lexi Buchanan brings you her new sexy standalone novel about fighting for freedom when the odds are against you.

LOVE STRYKER

EXCERPT

STRYKER (10 YEARS AGO)

"DAD, I'M NOT SURE this is such a good idea." My heart raced in my chest as though it would explode. My palms went slick as fear coursed through my veins.

I'd already thought Dad's late night plans were a bad idea...and they seemed worse the minute I saw the dark, deserted alley. It gave me the chills.

Nothing good was up that alley.

Even at fourteen I knew it, but my dad was determined so I followed him across the street. Something shouted for me to run, which gave me pause, but my legs had a mind of their own and followed him.

My dad turned, and then frowned when he noticed the slight hesitation in my usual eagerness to follow him anywhere. The nervous twitch in his right eye went crazy. "It isn't, but it's the only thing I can do."

Before I could work out what he meant, my dad grabbed my arm as though he was afraid I'd run. He dragged me to the mouth of what I considered a nightmare.

The stench of rotten food made me want to hurl. Every creak, even the wind howling around us, had my eyes constantly straining to see through the pitch black. I half expected someone to jump out brandishing a gun, or knife, or some other weapon.

Head down, my eyes landed on the hold my dad had on my arm. Something wasn't right. In fact, nothing about the evening felt right.

I knew my dad constantly bet on the fighters in the cage, winning and losing on a regular basis, but what that had to do with tonight, if anything, I didn't know. My dad never took me to the fights no matter how much I begged. I wanted to hang out with dad… wanted to be like the fighters—tough, strong, fearless. One day, that would be me standing in the cage with the crowds shouting my name. Then my dad wouldn't have any choice about keeping me away from that life.

I'd never understood the obsession my dad had for the fights, but they'd put him on a high for days afterwards…unless he lost.

Pulled to a stop, I felt the shake of my dad's hand as his grip tightened. He turned to look at me and the fear I saw in his eyes was something I'd never expected to see. My blood turned to ice and the wrongfulness of the night felt all too real as a large vehicle headed down the alley from the opposite entrance.

Caught in the headlights, my first reaction was to run and hide. The tension jumping off my dad was high. His breathing was frantic and sweat beaded on his forehead.

With my free hand, I shoved the black hood of my sweatshirt from my head so I didn't miss anything.

My pulse hammered in my neck and all I could hear was my heartbeat thrashing in my ears.

When my dad's only reaction was to stand and stare at the approaching vehicle, I knew then, that they where here because of him.

What had he done?

"Dad?" I turned and hoped he'd offer me an explanation as fear and anger knotted in my gut.

He didn't and wouldn't meet my gaze until the purr of the SUV's engine cut off. "Son, I'm sorry. If there was any other way I'd have taken it, but there isn't…I love you. You won't believe those words soon, but I mean them with every breath I take."

"What?"

Before he could say more, the doors of the SUV opened and a large man climbed out, moving behind us. Three other men emerged and stood in front.

The one in a dark suit stepped forward, his steely eyes on my dad. "Peter."

"Mr—"

"No names tonight…*Peter*." His gaze slid to me and my breath caught at the back of my throat. He looked me over—assessing. "He'll do."

What did he mean?

"Dad?"

My dad didn't explain and, seconds later, I felt his grip on my arm loosen as the large guy stepped closer.

None of this made any sense, but I'd known something was wrong the minute I'd stepped out of our apartment.

It was obvious that my dad had done, said, or agreed to something, but my brain worked overtime trying to work out just what.

Then I felt my wrists clasped tightly before they were pulled behind my back in a grip so strong that I knew even as I struggled that I wouldn't get free.

"Dad," I shouted, my eyes begged him to help me, but he just watched while they dragged me away.

The suit held his hand out and halted the guy who had me. He spoke with a threat inflected into his voice to my dad, "With this exchange, you can consider your debt paid in full. You stay away from him and me, and, you never step foot near the cage again…in any city. You won't like the consequences if you do." The man in the dark suit stepped in close to my dad, and threatened, "Am I clear?"

My dad's body quivered in fear and his eyes nearly bugged out of his head while the man threatened him.

Fear trickled from my belly and gradually spread throughout the more I listened to the conversation around me.

Until now, I had no idea just how serious my dad's gambling habit had become. I should have though. But surely he wasn't giving me over to the men to settle his debt. Was he? What did they want with me?

What... No!

The hold on me tightened as I started to struggle. The man behind me wasn't like the others. He was big and strong, and wore jeans and shirt as opposed to the others in suits. His scent was trouble, and even though I continued to struggle, I knew that he wouldn't release me.

My heart pounded as sweat ran down my face, mingling with the tears I couldn't control as my situation sank into my brain.

My dad, who I loved, who I thought loved me, had sold me in exchange for his gambling debt to be wiped clean. How could he do that?

My dad glanced at me one last time, pain in his eyes, before he turned and ran down the alley.

The man behind, tugged me toward a black SUV, but I struggled and tried to dig in my heels, my eyes still on my dad as he ran and left me with these assholes.

At the SUV, another man tried to grab my legs, but I kicked out and heard him curse as my booted foot slammed into the man's jaw.

"Hold that fucker," the man growled, grabbing me around the neck while more hands held me down.

My vision started to dim but then the man in

charge forcibly removed the hands. "I don't want the fucker dead." He stepped back straightening his jacket. "Get him in the truck. *Now.*"

No way!

In a last ditched effort to get away, I yelled, *"Dad! Help me!"*

My dad paused.

They all did.

Then my dad took one step toward me…hesitated. A bullet hissed from beside me—a silencer muffled the sound—and I watched as my dad disappeared around the corner seconds before I saw brick from the building fly off.

He did it!

He left me!

"I'm not going with you," I raged against every-thing. The fact of what my dad had done, the restraints holding my wrists, the hands gripping me. I struck out, blindly, as I struggled and kicked. My teeth sank into the soft flesh of the hand covering my mouth and I felt a moment of triumph as the man cursed in pain. Seconds later, the triumph was gone as the man's fist flew into my face. I felt the pain blossom, starting on my nose as my mouth filled with the metallic taste of blood. The pain ricocheted through me as I turned my head to the side and spat out blood. It felt like my jaw was on fire while I breathed through the pain.

I sucked in a breath to fight harder but my body tensed as fingers dug into my cheeks as a hand clamped around my face. The man in charge leaned forward, his eyes burning with anger as he loomed over me. "You're mine now lad. You're going to become my fighting machine. No more fucking nursemaids. I'm going to make you a man, and you're going to make me money to pay off your father's debt."

I couldn't talk with the hand clamped around me, but I memorized the man's face, and made sure that I would never forget it.

That close to me I noticed the scar to the right side of his face that ran a good few inches. I thought that he was an American at first, but now I wasn't sure. Something else was in him, and his accent, one I couldn't place, slipped with his anger.

I hoped that when I woke up in the morning the memory of tonight would still be there. Because one day, when I was a man—stronger—I was going to get even with everyone involved…including my dad, the one person I always thought would be there to love and support me—the one person who was supposed to protect me from evil.

How wrong was I?

EVIE (10 YEARS AGO)

WHILE MY MOM AND dad were partying with friends, and supporters of my father, I was on the sidelines trying to pretend my life didn't suck. I'd tried to fake a headache so I'd be allowed to stay home but it hadn't worked. I'd been told to sit and sip water regardless as to how late it had gotten.

I was twelve years old and hated that my father had just been elected as a state senator. My mother told me that I was selfish for thinking about myself all the time; that I should be more supportive.

How could I be more supportive when the new job meant my father would be away from home even more than he already had been? I really didn't see me wanting my dad at home as being selfish. I loved him, and missed him when he wasn't home.

But now, he would be gone more and school would be even harder to deal with. The other kids loved to make fun of me because of my family and my father's ambition.

I wanted to be part of a normal family. I couldn't even remember the last time we all ate around the table at the same time. I would only have my dad for family vacations now. He'd promised more but I knew that wouldn't happen. He loved his work, and really I should stop being ungrateful because I had everything I would ever want...apart from the one thing I *really* wanted...my father home.

My one best friend, Millie, was the only one who truly knew my fears, and she was the only person to know how much I hated my life.

Over the past few months I'd spent so much time at Millie's house that it felt like my second home. I loved being there. Her father was larger than life and, although he'd scared me at first, I'd finally gotten used to him.

My mother still tried to keep me apart from Millie when she wasn't lost in a world of her own making, and actually paid more attention as to what I was up to.

Like now.

I sighed as I spotted her walking toward me with a sour expression on her face, as though she'd eaten a lemon. It soon changed to a smile when Mrs. Grant appeared to her right.

Mom certainly had something on her mind though because her path continued toward me. I hated being center of attention, which she knew so I hoped that I wasn't expected on stage or anything while my father made his speech, even though I knew I wouldn't get away without.

"Evie dear." Mom took the cup of water from my hand and tugged me up. "Straighten your dress. Your father is about to make his speech and we both need to be at his side to show our support." And then she had to go and ruin it all. "We'll be on the front page of the newspaper tomorrow."

My heart sank and I wanted to run. I would have except her grip around my wrist tightened…almost to the point of being painful.

"Just be pleasant for the rest of the night, and," her lips twisted with annoyance, "I'll let you go on the trip with Millie and her family."

While her words sunk into my shocked brain, I let her lead me across the room to where my father stood with his team.

Mom knew how to get her way but I didn't for one minute believe she'd just thought about that to get me to do their bidding. She'd have something else up her sleeve and need me out of the way so that she didn't have a child to supervise. I wasn't about to complain because I wanted to go to Chicago with Millie more than anything. When I'd brought it up to Mom, she'd scoffed at the idea because she considered Millie's family beneath her. I couldn't see why she couldn't treat everyone the same.

"Smile," she hissed between her teeth.

And like the world's most lifelike puppet, I did exactly what she wanted. My smile was full of love and support as we greeted Father.

"There she is." His smile was real as he enclosed me in his warm embrace and I felt a pang of guilt that mine wasn't. "My princess," he whispered against my ear before he kissed the top of my head.

Available to purchase.

OTHER BOOKS BY AUTHOR

Hawke's Ridge

Maddox · Colton (2026)

Den Hollows

One of Six · Two of Six (2026)

Den of Filth (New MC Series 2025)

Reckless Wilder (2026)

Fifth Realm Series (Romantasy)

Quiver of Chaos · Wings & Arrows (2026)

Standalone Romantasy

Persephone Unchained

Tallulah James Mystery

*Dead and a Murder or Two · Dead and the Wedding Crashers ·
Dead and a Deadly Deed · Dead and a Best Friend*

Boston Bay Vikings

*Camden · Bennett · Ethan · Sutton · Carter · Bryson · Ivan · Theo
· Noah · Knox · Jericho · Roman*

Boston Bay Vikings Minor League

Lake · Rhodes · Nikoli · Dario · Madden · Bradford

Single Titles

Butterflies and Darkness · Come Back to Me · Indecent Villain · Lawful · Love Stryker · Tears in the Rain · Whispers of Yesterday

Holiday Season

Holiday Kisses in the Snow · Jingle Bells

Romantic Suspense Series

Twenty Eight Days · The Next Victim (2025)

Blossom Creek

Christmas at Emelia's · A Rake in Blossom Creek · Heatwave in Blossom Creek · Secret Love in Blossom Creek · Mischief in Blossom Creek · Runaway Bride in Blossom Creek · Naughty & Nice in Blossom Creek

Bad Boy Rockers

My Brother's Girl · Past Sins · My Best Friend's Sister · Never Let Go · Saving Jace · Silent Night (Novella)

Kincaid Sisters

Meant to be Mine · You Were Always Mine · Will You be Mine

McKenzie Brothers

Playing with the Boss · A McKenzie Wedding (Novella) · Playing with Fire · Playing with Desire · Playing with Trouble · Playing with their Hearts · A McKenzie Christmas (Novella)

De La Fuente Family (McKenzie Spinoff)

Love in Montana · Love in Purgatory · Love in Bloom · Love in Country · Love in Flame · Love in Game · Love in Education

McKenzie Cousins

(McKenzie Spinoff)

Baby Makes Three · A Business Decision · Secret Kisses · Kissing Cousins · If Only · Princess & the Puck · A Bakers Delight · A Cowboy for Christmas · A Secret Affair · One Christmas · The Pregnant Professor · It Started with a Kiss

Novella's

Educate Me · One Dance · Pure

ABOUT THE AUTHOR

While Lexi is the author of the chick lit series, Tallulah James Mystery, and the fantasy/romance series, The Fifth Realm, she is also the author of over seventy novels. Based in Ireland, this British author has been writing since 2013.

Follow on social media:

Website: http://lexibuchanan.net
Email: authorlexibuchanan@gmail.com

facebook.com/lexibuchananauthor
x.com/AuthorLexi
instagram.com/authorlexib
bookbub.com/author/lexi-buchanan
amazon.com/Lexi-Buchanan/e/B009SPA94U